SHORTSTOP ON WHEELS

By the author of

SHORTSTOP

By JOE ARCHIBALD

ON WHEELS

Macrae Smith Company: Philadelphia

SHORTSTOP ON WHEELS

1

SOUND, LACED WITH BOOS AND TAUNTING laughter, cascaded out of the stands when the tall and stringy kid with flaming red hair stepped up to the plate to hit for the Grafton Rockets. The boy's shoulders sagged under it, and a few moments later he stood at the plate with his eyes on the ground and let a good pitch go by. Out at shortstop for the Hagersville Ponies, little Howie Patton ground his teeth and wondered who was more grown up in this ball park, the Little Leaguers or the adults looking on. Before the start of this important regional game, a few grownups had acted like spoiled brats, protesting the eligibility of the redhead now at bat.

Howie moved back a few feet, for Terry Nolan could really club the ball. Nolan was twelve years old, but he looked at least fourteen, and overrabid local fans questioned the date on his birth certificate, certain it was made out long after he was born.

Alfie Crowell, pitching for the Ponies, threw two pitches wide of the plate, then served one up that was hit like a bullet inches outside third.

A voice yelled, "Back more, Howie! Move back!" The little shortstop wished his father had stayed at home. Ever since the first inning he had been yelling at his son, his powerful voice easily distinguished from those of nearly four thousand other fans. Howie knew Clary McCue, the Ponies' manager, did not like it either. In direct contrast to the kid at the plate, Howie Patton was small for his age, but grim determination and a fast pair of legs had compensated, thus far, for lack of muscle. He was halfway between ten and eleven years but looked no more than eight or nine.

Alfie Crowell took his time delivering a two and two pitch, so Howie tipped his cap back and let air wash over his brown hair now soaking wet from the July heat. He had a habit of nudging his slightly upturned nose with the first knuckle of his thumb. When Crowell wound up he got set, trying to ignore the crowd's heckling of Terry Nolan. Alfie threw low, into the dirt, running the count to three and two, and a man shouted, "Walk the ringer, kid! Don't let him hit it!"

More than a few fans roared their disapproval of the heckler. Howie grinned. Always in a barrel there are some sour apples. He leaned forward, hands on his knees, when Crowell fired again. The redhead swung, drove the ball between center and right, and came into second standing up. Hagersville fans lost a lot of steam. This was the first scoring threat by either team. It was the top of the fifth and only one more inning left to play. This was the game that would decide the regional championship; the winner would be well on the way to Williamsport.

"Come on, Alfie, burn it by him!" Howie shouted, when the next hitter dug in. Crowell threw a strike across, then a ball. The third pitch came back to Howie on one hop, and he threw the runner out. "Only two more, Alfie," he piped at the little left-hander. The Pony fans came back to life when the next batter lofted a pop fly behind third, close to the foul line, then turned loose a cry of dismay when the third baseman let it pop out of his glove. Nolan, however, stayed on second, sure the ball would be caught. There was still only one out and Rockets were on first and second. Alfie Crowell, a quick-tempered youngster, glared at his third baseman before he started working on the next hitter.

Howie shouted, "He feels worse than you do, Alfie. Throw it!"

Crowell tried a sweeping curve. It broke wide of the plate, eluding the Pony catcher. Both Rocket base runners advanced, while the crowd implored the Rockets to keep going. Alfie kicked dirt up from the hill when Howie trotted in from short to cool him off. The crowd was on Alfie. Most of them screamed for McCue to drag him out. Howie heard his father yell, "What are you waiting for, McCue?"

A small Negro boy, white teeth flashing, stepped up to hit when young Crowell toed the rubber again. He lashed at the first pitch and hit a bleeder that rolled between third and the pitcher's mound. Alfie raced to his right and scooped the ball up, then froze when he saw he had no chance to make a play. The big redhead scored from third with the game's first run, and Rocket supporters rose up, shouting with delight. They turned loose a more deafening racket when the next batter hit a clean single over second to score Grafton's second run.

Manager McCue made his move. Alfie walked off the diamond, his head down, tears in his eyes, the boos and catcalls from some of the spectators adding to his misery. Then bigger trouble broke loose as Ray Stott came in from left field to take over the pitching chores. A big man in a brown shirt came out of the stands, evaded the grasp of a special policeman, and rushed at McCue just as the Ponies' manager put an arm over Alfie's shoulder preparatory to walking the boy to the bench.

"We'll protest this game, McCue," the man roared. Howie and several other Ponies converged near the pitcher's mound, their eyes wide with shock. "That redhead doesn't belong in the Little League! I help support the Ponies with my dough, and I'm not going to let the Grafton crowd get away with this!"

9

For another fifteen minutes the two competing Little League teams stood by aghast, watching a milling group of adults slip back into second childhood. They were dismayed and confused, most of them remembering the rules of conduct impressed upon them by their elders and the punishments they sustained when those rules were broken. They watched the big man in the brown shirt and several of his supporters throw punches at those who tried to restore order, and they were fearful that this hassle would put an end to Little League ball in Hagersville.

Ray Stott, something of a comic, bounced the ball up and down in his glove and laughed nervously. "I'll bet my father can lick your father," he said to Willie Abendroth, the Ponies' squat little catcher.

"Maybe," Willie replied, "but I bet he couldn't lick my mother."

Howie grinned a little as he watched three other policemen move in and break up the disturbance. The Little Leaguers broke apart when the instigators were unceremoniously hustled out of the ball park. Howie, still shaken, walked back to his position, and the plate umpire called out, above the subdued racket in the stands, "Play ball!"

Waiting for Stott to pitch to his first batter, Howie heard his father again. "Come on, get 'em out!" the bass voice implored. He got set, wishing the officials would also limit the age of the fans who watched Little League competition. Did people ever grow up? Stott's second delivery came back at him like a shot, and he dug it out of the dirt and got the force at second. Mickey Shea pivoted nicely and fired to first to complete a double play, and the Ponies came running in to take their cuts.

McCue's peanut-sized players managed to get a run by virtue of a single, an error, and a double by Ray Stott. The Hagersville side took heart once more and gave the Ponies a rousing cheer when the team took the field again.

10

"Boot one and they'll dust our pants," Mickey Shea threw at Howie, as they waited for Stott to throw. "I'm goin' to be awful short of spendin' money if we lose."

Howie nodded to himself. He had heard the talk in Hagersville about the undue pressure competitive baseball put on adolescents. It led to something known as frustration, and it seeded various complexes in young minds. He was too young to grasp such complexities, and he certainly felt no different since he'd first swung a bat on an empty lot next to Sugden's lumberyard. Grownups could find more stuff to worry a little guy who was well satisfied with his small world.

Ray Stott set the spectators buzzing by striking out the first two Rockets to face him. He got the third hitter on a pop-up that Howie took in short left after quite a run, and the fans came up off the seats yelling for the Ponies to draw even. Mickey Shea responded by banging a hit off the Rocket third sacker's glove and took second, when the opposing left fielder fumbled the ball close to the foul line as he raced in to pick it up.

The hecklers on the Grafton side sharpened their needles as Howie stepped up to the plate. He heard his father's deep voice. "Get hold of it, Howie. Get a good one. Don't swing at anything!"

"One out!" a fan shouted.

Howie was hitless up to now, in this game. At the plate he regretted his lack of power. The bat felt heavy in his hands when the first pitch blazed in. He had to step back in a hurry, but the ball grazed the letters on the front of his shirt and he was waved to first. There was a mild protest from the Rockets' catcher, but the umpire stared him out of countenance and snapped, "All right, son, play ball!"

Ollie Halgren, the first baseman, and Joey Brigante, the Ponies' center fielder, flied out, and the Hagersville crowd began to squirm and put verbal pressure on their little team.

Taking a lead off first with Vince Gorman at bat, Howie shuttled back and forth, trying to draw a throw that could be wild. One thing he *could* do was run. Vince was the Pony left fielder who had taken over for Stott, and a pretty good hitter. He tagged the Rockets' pitcher for a line drive that hit behind first base just inside the foul line. Mickey Shea streaked around and scored and Howie, the crowd's noise drowning out a warning cry from the third-base coach, did not stop at third. He dashed for the plate, his little legs moving like pistons. The relay from the outfield banged into the Grafton catcher's mitt when Howie was ten feet from the plate, then bounced out. Howie came across with the leading run, feeling sorry for the Rockets' catcher.

Clary McCue was both elated and displeased. "You should have been out, Howie," he said, when the shortstop approached the bench. "A goat instead of a hero. Didn't you hear?"

"No, Mr. McCue," Howie said honestly. "All I heard was my dad yelling for me to keep running."

"Yeah," McCue bit out, glaring at the seats back of third. "We've got more than a dozen managers here." He shrugged, turned, cupped his hands over his mouth, and yelled to the boy at the plate. "Get the one you like, Willie!"

Willie Abendroth took a ball, hit a long foul, then bounced out to the pitcher.

Ray Stott, in the top of the sixth, got the first Grafton batter out on a fly to center. The Hagersville fans turned loose a great roar when he struck out the Grafton first baseman. They began moving toward the runways, certain that the Ponies would reach Williamsport. A few moments later the crack of a bat froze them in their tracks. The Rockets' right fielder was trotting around the bases and, out in center field, Joey Brigante was watching the ball sail over the fence. The score was tied!

12

Stott fanned the next hitter, but the damage had been done. Little Ray Stott never lifted his eyes all the way to the Ponies' bench. Some of the fans rode him hard.

Grafton put a new pitcher in, a lean eleven-year-old who set the Ponies down in order.

Going into extra innings, McCue stayed with Stott, and the towhead also mowed the opposition down, one, two, three.

In the eighth, the Rockets' right fielder slammed a double to left, after one man was out, and advanced to third, while Mickey Shea threw out the next hitter after making a sparkling stop between first and second. Stott got the next batter to hit a high pop to shallow center and Joey Brigante raced in, the crowd heaving a huge sigh of relief. Joey got the ball in his glove, then dropped it, and the Rocket outfielder raced home with the tie-breaking run.

The little center fielder was a picture of deep despair when he came in from the field a few minutes later. Howie said, "Forget it. We'll get even, Joey."

"The sun got in my eyes, honest," Joey said.

There was a sullenness in the quiet of the Hagersville fans that reached the Ponies' bench. The largely adult crowd felt the kids had given up on them. McCue said, when Vince Gorman stepped up to hit, "We've got three outs left. We can still win."

Vince took a strike, two balls, then tied into the pitch he was looking for and rifled it to deep right for a double. The Pony rooters came up out of the doldrums and yelled for victory again. Joey's error forgotten, the crowd yelled at the top of their lungs for him when he beat out a slow roller down the first-base line, sending Gorman to third. The Grafton manager yanked his pitcher and brought in a southpaw, a stocky youngster named Merullo.

Merullo struck out the next Pony player and followed up by fanning Mickey Shea. Howie stepped up to the plate, the

13

heavy burden on his frail shoulders. Fans shouted at Clary McCue to trot out another hitter. The little shortstop heard his father yelling at him. "Remember what I've kept telling you, Howie. Don't try to kill the ball, just meet it!"

Tony Merullo, from Grafton, looked in at Howie and grinned slowly. He chewed furiously on his gum, then nodded at his catcher. He threw one down the middle, just above the knees, and Howie swung hard and missed. "Good-bye, Williamsport!" a stout-lunged fan yelled.

Howie stepped out and got dirt on his hands. His legs were shaking when he planted the corrugated soles of his sneakers near the plate and looked out at the pitcher. He let a bad pitch go by, then dribbled the next offering foul a few feet from the plate. "One more!" the Grafton catcher called out to Merullo when he fired the ball back. "That one they can't see!"

"Stay in there, Howie!" It was his father's voice and its timbre told him it was a stern order, not encouragement. He waited, his teeth grinding together. The pitch came in, a curve that swept wide, and he refused to bite.

"Wait him out, kid!" a man shouted. "Get a walk!"

Merullo rubbed the ball up and let Howie wait, having watched a lot of big leaguers work. He glanced at the base runners, then cut loose without a windup. Howie held off, certain that the pitch was a little high. The umpire agreed. Howie sucked in his breath and got ready for the payoff pitch. Merullo glared at the umpire for a moment before he went back to work. He nodded at a sign from his catcher, then fired hard. The ball seemed to come straight toward Howie, and he leaned back. Suddenly it broke in and over, cutting the heart of the plate. The umpire emphatically gave the strike sign, then walked away. The Grafton players were rushing toward each other while Howie still stood at the plate, not daring for a moment to turn away and see the woebegone expressions on the faces of his teammates.

The fans were pouring out onto the field when he trudged

14

toward the bench, fathers singling out their sons. He saw big Mike Abendroth, a Hagersville contractor, put a hand on his son's shoulder and heard him say, "It isn't the end of the world, Willie. We'll get 'em next year, huh? You still got a year of Little League ball."

Howie looked around for a sign of his father as he ran toward the locker room of Hagersville's stadium with Mickey Shea and Joey Brigante. Joey's eyes were blinking hard and not because of the sun. "I muffed it, not you, Howie," Joey said.

Howie was peeling off in the dressing room when his father came in. H.L. Patton possessed the physique he wished he had passed on to his son. He had a heavy-browed blocky face, a pair of sharp slate-gray eyes, and a stubborn impatience with ineptness. He also had the reputation of being the worst loser ever to rent a locker at the Hagersville country club.

"I'm sorry, dad," Howie said, over a lump in his throat, and dropped his eyes to the cement floor.

"You should be. You looked pretty silly standing there with your bat on your shoulder. Those other kids ought to take you over to the lake and throw you in." The elder Patton clamped his teeth over a cold pipe and looked at his son as if he had just crawled out of the woodwork. "I always knew I was wasting time teaching you how to play baseball. I think you'd better take up something else, Howie, like table tennis!"

Howie's head snapped up when he heard Clary McCue's voice. "Now wait a minute, Patton. You're going at this all cock-eyed, like a lot of other people in this town. The boy feels bad enough, but he'll forget it all tomorrow if you'll just leave him alone."

"This is my kid, McCue!" Patton snapped. "He's no longer your business, is that clear?"

"Sure, Harry, it means you're taking him out of the Little League."

"He's no ballplayer, McCue, and you know it!"

15

Rocco Brigante was talking to his son, kidding him, asking what was so important about winning. He finally got a snicker out of Joey and he winked at Ollie Halgren's father. Halgren said, "They played great but had bad luck."

Howie suddenly got up and threw a sneaker against the door of a locker. His eyes stormy and glistening with tears, he faced his father. His chin was high and thrust out and his hands were balled into fists. For everyone within earshot to hear, he shouted, "I'll be a ballplayer no matter what you say or do, no matter how you try to stop me! Some day you'll be sorry you were ashamed of me!"

As he turned and ran out of the dressing room, McCue smiled thinly and said, "Patton, I think you will."

Supper at the Patton home that night was anything but enjoyable. Howie's mother was aware that the ever-widening rift between father and son was one that even time might never heal.

When Howie shook his head at the offer of a second piece of his favorite cherry pie, Harry Patton banged his water glass down. "How long are you going to sulk?" he asked.

"I'm not sulking," Howie said. "I just haven't got anything to say you want to hear." He pushed his chair back. "May I be excused?" His mother nodded, and he hurried out of the room and went upstairs, where he sat down on the edge of his bed and feasted his eyes on the framed photographs of big league ballplayers covering one small wall of his room. Although unaware of it, his choice of heroes past and present was deeply significant. They were all men of comparatively small stature who had gained fame without the ability to hit the long ball or compile a .300 batting average. They had the knack of getting on base one way or another so that the muscle men could drive them in. They could hit the old-fashioned singles and lay down the good bunt seven times out of ten. They were great glove men, and the ones who stole the bases.

16

Howie had picked up a dog-eared record book he had bought for a dollar and stretched out on the bed to absorb more vital statistics when he heard a car in front. It had to be Sam McCloud because he always stopped on a dime, making his tires squeal. Howie's spirits rose. Sam McCloud was one of Hagersville's most famous citizens, having played eight years in the outfield of a big league club. Sam had retired and invested in a restaurant and bowling alley. For the past four years he had coached the Ponies and had been their original sponsor.

Howie walked out to the stair landing, about to call to Sam, then checked himself. He guessed it would be smart to keep out of the way for a while.

"How's things, Harry?" McCloud asked, when the front door closed behind him. "I just got in from Rutland. I hoped I'd get back in time for the game, but I got tied up."

"You didn't miss a thing, Sam. The kids played a sloppy game and handed it to Grafton on a platter."

"I heard different on the car radio," McCloud replied, his voice a little sharp. "Two extra innings. So the boys made errors. They boot them in the majors, too. In my book they put up a fine battle, and I'm proud of them."

"You didn't have a kid out there, Sam. It makes a difference. Howie could have tied it up with any kind of a bloop hit. He just stood there and. . . ."

The voice trailed off as the two men moved out of the hall and into the living room. Lips tight, Howie moved halfway down the stairs, careful of the one riser that always groaned underfoot. Leaning against the banister he could see part of the front room, including a clear view of Sam McCloud's hawkish profile. There were swatches of gray at his temples and his face still had the leathery toughness of an active big leaguer in mid-August. He was forty-eight, a confirmed bachelor.

"You'd better not blame the kids if they kill Little League

17

ball here, Harry," McCloud said. "The ruckus full-grown men put up before and during that game was disgraceful."

"A lot of kids here don't have the temperament or the talent for the game, Sam," Harry Patton argued. "Howie's batting two hundred and thirty-one, way down in the list of Little League hitters. He——"

"Harry," McCloud said, with some impatience, "it wasn't really Howie you were watching today—or any other day. You saw yourself, at the boy's age. You created the image of yourself because you regret there was no Little League when you were a boy. You weren't looking at reality but at an illusion. Howie did not live up to the hero's role you imagined for yourself. The great majority of those kids will take their disappointment in stride, but some of the fathers will stew over it for weeks to come. Losing is a personal insult and their pride is hurting."

Harry Patton laughed a little scornfully. "If you want to analyze me, Sam, let me stretch out on the couch. I'll still say the trouble with Little League baseball here is that there are too few boys in the area to draw from. There are only half a dozen with enough talent to meet the competition from bigger places."

"They came close to going to Williamsport," McCloud reminded him. "One error was the difference. Who has a right to demand perfection in anything? I'm fed up to my gums with this talk about putting pressure on the kids. Is it worse for a boy to go up to bat in front of three or four thousand people and strike out than it is for him to face an auditorium full of adults and let him recite the 'Wreck of the Hesperus'? Frustration, my foot, Harry! A boy meets frustration from the time he's born, when his bottle falls out of his crib and he can't reach it, when he finds he's scared to climb high enough up a tree where there's a nest full of bird's eggs, when he knows he can't have the brand-new bicycle in the store window. Sure,

18

the kids have tender feelings, but it doesn't help them when adults keep rubbing them raw."

"Yeah, Sam. Why is it that people who never have kids of their own set themselves up as experts on child psychology?"

"Maybe because guys like me see boys precisely as they are, without idealization, without parental bias," Sam McCloud said. "We see them as distinct individuals with minds and ambitions of their own. More often than not, we stress their virtues rather than their faults. I think the game today proved that the parents in Hagersville, not the kids, are not ready for Little League baseball."

"You tell that to the people in this town, Sam, and you'll get your ears pinned back."

"I'll risk it, Harry." McCloud got out of his chair and looked up at the ceiling. "Howie up there? Do you mind if I have a few words with him?"

"Go right ahead, Sam. When you come down, Grace will have some coffee ready."

Howie slipped back up the stairs and went into his room. He seemed very much absorbed in a book when McCloud rapped on his door, then slowly swung it open.

The former star gave him a broad grin. "That must have been quite a pitch you looked at, Howie," he said.

The boy had to laugh. "Mr. McCloud, it was the sweetest curve I ever saw," he said. He was surprised how good he felt, admitting it. "I'm dead sure Mickey Shea would have struck out on it, too." A small smile played on his wide mouth for a fleeting instant. "But—but Dad's right, I guess. I'll never be much of a ballplayer."

McCloud sat down on the bed beside Howie, his eyes wandering over the boy's picture gallery. "Would you let me be the judge of that, Howie?" he said. He stabbed a finger at the wall. "That guy there. One of the best, Howie. He weighed a hundred and sixty-two pounds and was five foot six and a half. He hit .257, but he scored more runs than any other player on the club. He stole fifty-one bases last year and drew the most walks. Would you say he wasn't much of a ballplayer?"

"You think I could be anywhere near as good, Mr. McCloud?"

"That's entirely up to you, Howie."

"I'd have to keep playing ball. If they do away with the Little League here, I won't get much of a chance."

McCloud threw a long arm around Howie. "Let me worry about that, boy."

"I'm pretty small and spindly and might never grow too tall. They take hitters in the big leagues nowadays," Howie said dolefully. "My dad could be right, Mr. McCloud."

"And he could be wrong." Sam McCloud got up and walked the limited confines of the room. "Let me tell you something, Howie. By the time you're old enough to play regular ball, I'm pretty certain that radical changes in the game will have been made. The show will be taken away from the muscle men who have been making a farce out of baseball. Fans come to see visiting sluggers hit the long ones and don't care a hang whether the home team wins or loses. Show me a game other than baseball where the dimensions of the playing field differ! Oh, the writers and the other experts point out that it is impossible to reconstruct old ball parks, and I'll admit they're right. But they can establish ground rules to abolish the Chinese homers hit down the short foul lines."

Howie said, "Yeah, Mr. McCloud. It doesn't seem right to me. I've watched a lot of games on TV where hitters drive the ball well over four hundred feet and only get a long out. Seems if you learn to pull you're a home-run hitter."

McCloud nodded. "They've made some ball parks to order for certain hitters. I wouldn't allow any man a home run if

20

he hit a ball less than four hundred feet. And the ball, Howie —don't let them tell you it isn't hopped up and that the seams aren't nearly flush with the horsehide covering."

"I guess the fans want the homers, Mr. McCloud, and they would kick about changing the rules."

"Don't kid yourself, son. When well over a thousand home runs are hit every year in the two big leagues, the fans are going to be fed up before long. They'll want to see a man who can run bases like Ty Cobb used to or see a bunt laid down. They'll cheer the guy who can get an old-fashioned single when it is needed. You mark my word, it'll happen. Baseball will return to sanity, and the home-run sideshow will fizzle out. You be ready."

"I'll try, Mr. McCloud." This was hope dashed to earth and rising again.

McCloud picked up a book from Howie's bed table and flipped the pages. "The great mogul ball park!" he exclaimed. "Two hundred and ninety-six feet down the right-field foul line, three hundred and one down the left-field line. How many line drives have gone into that Inner Mongolia, Howie?" He kept turning pages. "Here's one: three hundred and nine feet down the right-field line, a paradise for pull hitters, chronic pull hitters who couldn't hit to another field once in twenty tries. If a lot of them had been born a lot sooner, son, they couldn't have carried Ty Cobb's suitcase. And it doesn't make sense to say the ball isn't livelier than it was twenty or twenty-five years ago. I knew stronger men than those hitting them into the seats today. They couldn't build up a dozen home runs."

"It does seem funny," the boy admitted, McCloud's every word having built up the courage he had lost earlier in the afternoon. He hoped the ex-big leaguer's words would prove prophetic.

As young as he was, it occurred to him that maybe Sam McCloud had been a little overcritical of the modern game, maybe secretly stewing over an unenviable record as a home-run hitter. Anyway, Howie thought, that was what his father would have said. He couldn't help asking.

"You hit many, Mr. McCloud?"

The big man grinned. "I know what you're thinking, Howie. I hit thirteen my last year. Never could pull a ball worth a lick, but I backed a lot of outfielders against the fences, mostly in center. Well, I've got to run along, but I'll be in touch." He put a hand on Howie's head and rumpled the boy's brown hair. You know something? I always get a kick out of doing a thing that seems impossible. I'm going to make a real ball-player out of you."

They went downstairs together. Howie felt the atmosphere was a little less strained.

When Sam McCloud finished his coffee and pulled a cigar from his breast pocket, he said, "Thanks, Grace. When you decide you don't want Howie any longer, just give me a ring."

"You'll wait forever, Sam," Mrs. Patton said, laughing a little. Harry Patton seemed just a trifle abashed, but he managed a grin.

On TV that night Howie and his father watched the Moguls overcome a five-run Boston Blues lead in the eighth and ninth, a home run that hit the foul pole in right being the deciding blow. Harry Patton said, "I have to admit it's ridiculous. That ball didn't travel over three hundred and twenty feet. Well, if I was a pitcher in that league I'd look for a job somewhere else."

"Mr. McCloud said there are four teams in the majors that would have a hard time winning from good minor league teams," Howie said, and his father nodded in agreement.

Their dreams of playing in Williamsport, Pennsylvania, in August having burst like so many bubbles, most of the Little

22

Leaguers in Hagersville became fully resigned to the obscurity of the big vacant lot behind Sam McCloud's restaurant and bowling alley. "It could've been worse," Willie Abendroth said, just before they chose up sides. "We could've gone into the semifinals and got beat, which would've been so near, yet so far. O.K., Alfie, you pitch for our side."

Sam McCloud joined the boys just as the Mudcats came in to take their cuts in the last of the fourth. He sat down on a wooden bench and watched Vince Gorman hit. Vince had two strikes against him when McCloud walked over to him and corrected his stance. "Feet wider apart, Vince, and choke up on that bat a little."

Vince clubbed the next pitch for a hit, and Howie, out at short for the Tigers, grinned. His face beamed.

McCloud went back and sat down, a small smile crackling the crows' feet around his eyes. These kids had accepted their setback gracefully, but the adults in Hagersville were still growling. He'd just come from Rotary, and the words of one of the members still rang in his head. "Let's hope that Grafton team gets clobbered at Williamsport. I still say they had two kids on that team at least thirteen years old."

McCloud leaned forward, abstractedly watching the play. His mind was on grown men who sometimes wore squirt-bulb flowers in their buttonholes and handed out trick cigars or tore up furniture in convention hotels. There were too many of these "grownup boys" in a world desperately in need of maturity.

A few weeks later, after the Grafton Rockets had become the Little League champions, the officials and sponsors of the Hagersville Ponies met at the Y.M.C.A. and voted against continuing Little League activity for at least two years.

23

2

DURING THE NEXT TWO SUMMERS, SAM MC-
Cloud was Mr. Baseball in Hagersville. He took care of most
of the expense involved, including the chartering of buses to
take his twelve-to-fifteen-year-old kids to play teams in other
towns. He gave particular attention during the practice ses-
sions to Howie, Willie Abendroth, and Ray Stott, for they
looked like future professional ballplayers. Howie had grown
an inch and a half since the last Little League game he'd
played, and his shoulders were broader, but he was still no
dangerous long-ball hitter. McCloud admired Howie's hustle,
his ability to get walks, and the amount of ground he covered
at shortstop.

"You watch him," McCloud said to a group of onlookers,
one evening in July when the days were long. "The boy really
has the *wheels.*" He grinned. "I mean legs. They can be the
difference between a .230 and a .290 hitter."

Two teams were playing five innings, the Bugs and the
Crickets. Howie was up swinging a bat with two balls and one
strike on him.

McCloud saw Howie give a sign to a little base runner taking a short lead off first, so he walked up to the plate, calling
for time. "This isn't the time for the hit and run, Howie. You

should know that. The only legitimate hit and run situation is when the count is three balls and one strike. The pitcher's hands are tied; he must throw a strike or give the hitter a base on balls."

"I guess I forgot, Mr. McCloud," Howie said. A few minutes later, with the runner going, he blooped a hit into short right, sending the base runner to third.

McCloud stopped the game a few minutes later to correct Willie Abendroth's position back of the plate. "You've got to have your body well balanced in the crouch, Willie: your knees rather close together, your bare hand close to the body on the inside of the leg. Keep your mitt placed over the other knee in a comfortable position. See, like this!"

As far as McCloud was concerned, the play on this sandlot revolved around Howie Patton. He kept his eye on the boy every minute. In the fourth, the youngster playing first for the Bugs slammed a double into right field. Howie stood and watched the relay from the outfield go through the second baseman. By the time the ball was retrieved, the base runner was perched on third. McCloud called Howie over to the base line near third. "You knew better than that," he said, a little impatiently. "You were supposed to back second up on that throw."

"I'll remember," Howie said, his ears a little red.

"I'll stop by your house about nine thirty tomorrow, Howie. We can get in a couple of hours of work, mostly on bunting. O.K.?"

"O.K.," the boy said.

Driving away from the lot in McCloud's car, Howie said, "They're still going for the home runs in the big leagues. Nothing has changed much so far, Mr. McCloud."

"Changes take plenty of time. The fans still have some appetite for the homers, but they'll get too many before long. Reminds me of the man who lost a bet that he could eat a quail a day for thirty days. At the end of the third week he gave up and swore he didn't want to see another one of those game birds as long as he lived. Lots of things enter into it, Howie. The plate umpires have narrowed the strike zone, and the pitchers can't use the shine ball or the emery ball. How many modern pitchers win twenty games in a season?"

"Well, it won't make any difference in my hitting," Howie said, laughing, "no matter what they do to the ball, Mr. McCloud!"

Harry Patton came off the porch when McCloud stopped in front of his house. Howie knew his father was steaming by the way he slammed the newspaper down. The smell of newly cut grass suddenly reminded him of a chore he'd forgotten to do.

"I was going to mow the lawn first thing in the morning," he said, fast, when he got out of the car, but his father's displeasure was directed toward McCloud.

"Would it be asking too much, Sam, if you'd just let me have a little supervision over my own kid? He has chores to do. Baseball, baseball! He sleeps and eats it. What'll he be at twenty-one when he finds out he's no ballplayer? A lazy loafer!"

"Howie," McCloud said, "you never told me you had grass to cut. From now on you attend to those things first."

"I'll do the talking to him, Sam," Patton snapped. "He doesn't play ball for a week and he gets no allowance for two weeks."

"Quite a tough fine," McCloud said, smiling only with his mouth. "You'd make a tough umpire, Harry." He started toward his car, then swung around. "But more lawn mowing wouldn't hurt you a bit, friend; you're building a spare tire around your middle."

Harry Patton, failing to come up with a suitable reply, sputtered, and waved Howie into the house.

26

Up in his room, Howie thought of the punishment he'd received. No allowance meant the purchase of the new infielder's glove he'd spotted would have to be delayed, but he guessed being kept away from the baseball diamond for a week would be the hardest thing to bear. Suspended, he told himself, and brightened up again. He felt like a big leaguer who had bumped an umpire. Sure, it was all part of the game.

Howie sighed, nudged his nose with a thumb knuckle, reached for a hard-cover book, *Baseball and Team Strategy*, and turned to the chapter devoted to shortstops. For the hundredth time he studied it, stowing away in his mind the plays expected of a shortstop under varying situations, particularly the one where a shortstop must guard against a bunt when men are on first and second. The book said the shortstop had the most important fielding position, had to be capable of making plays in a wide range of territory, had to have a strong throwing arm and be able to throw accurately with either a side-arm or an overhand movement. He had to be quick in his body motions, with a razor-sharp brain to anticipate plays.

It never did much good, McCloud had told him, to read about batting in a book. Oh, there were certain faults that could be corrected, but most good hitters were born, not made. If a man has the strength he can swing a bat by the extreme end, but the small players for the most part do better holding the bat far up the handle and swinging with a short stroke.

When Howie went downstairs to catch his favorite private eye adventure on television, his father put his book down and studied him for a long moment, a gleam of satisfaction in his eyes. "I met John Trenk on the street this morning, Howie. You know, Sid's father?"

The boy nodded. The Trenks had moved away to White River a year ago. Sid had been quite a ballplayer for Hagersville High, and had been given a bonus after graduation to sign with a major league club.

"Sid's home, his father told me, and fed up," Patton went on. "Two years of being kicked around in the Class D leagues where, he said, one kid in a thousand might catch the eye of a big-league scout. All Sid got out of the game was a bad stomach and an aversion to professional baseball. He's going to take what money he has left and study electronics."

"Yeah?" Howie said, immune to discouragement at his early age. "Sid was a first baseman who could hit, but he never could pick low ones out of the dirt. He was the worst fielding first baseman in the high school league and had an awful temper. If he hadn't hit a lot of homers they wouldn't have paid any attention to him."

"I suppose the big-league scouts will line up to get your name on a contract," Harry Patton said.

His wife gestured with impatience and put her fancy work aside. "It's silly, Harry, the way you argue with Howie about baseball. He's still too young to know his own mind. In a couple of years he'll most likely forget baseball and want to be an astronaut."

"He's got the build for it," Howie's father said dryly. "You could put two of him in the capsules they're using today."

Howie forgot his favorite TV program. Angry tears burning his eyes, he walked out of the room and out of the house, slamming the door behind him. Always his father reminded him of his smallness, his shortcomings. He was too small to go on fishing trips but strong enough to push a lawn mower; too small to have a boat but big enough to wash and polish the family car. Someday, he promised himself as he circled the block, even if he never grew much more than average size, he would be big. He just had to be. It might take years, but there would come a day when he'd make some big men feel mighty small.

28

"McCloud called up," his father told him, when he returned to the house. "He's arranged a game with some kids from Fairlee next Saturday morning. You can play if you like."

Howie wondered for a moment if his ears were playing tricks with him. Finally he grinned and said, "Gee, thanks!" His conscience pricked him a little, and he started wondering if he had magnified past grievances, as he went to the kitchen to see if any of the chocolate cake was left. It wasn't until late the next day that he learned the real reason for his father's generosity. Harry Patton's outboard motor was out of whack and he needed McCloud's. McCloud needed a shortstop, so it was a good deal all around.

Howie was sorely tempted to throw a monkey wrench into the whole deal by refusing to play, but the love of the game of baseball was too strong inside him. It was just something else he must remember not to forget.

It wasn't a smiling little shortstop that took the field for McCloud's Ponies when the umpire called "Play ball!" on Saturday morning. Howie's eyes were stormy and he seethed within, the taunts from one of the Fairlee players, thrown at him during the short practice session, still ringing in his ears. "That shrimp on your team, McCloud?" the Fairlee Duke first baseman had shouted. "He looks like a glove wearin' a kid!"

"That guy's name is Bolavshanski," Willie Abendroth had told Howie. "He's a freshman in high school."

Howie believed it. He was the biggest kid on the field and looked as if he owned it.

The Duke leadoff man swung at Ray Stott's second pitch and drove it on one hop to Howie, who threw his man out easily. Number two hitter fanned, but the Dukes' center fielder rifled the ball to deep left for three bases. That brought Bolavshanski up, and the Pony fielders moved back, Howie going out on the grass. The big blond boy with the wide-toothed smile watched two bad pitches go by.

"He's afraid, Boly," a Duke bench jockey called out. "He'll walk you."

"Yeah," the batter shouted. "He's all chicken!"

Ray Stott reared back and fired. The batter swung and connected, a blistering line drive that Howie jumped high for and caught in the webbing of his glove. Bolavshanski slammed his bat down and glared at Howie as the Pony shortstop trotted toward the bench.

For three innings the Ponies battled even with the highly favored visitors, 4-4. Two of Fairlee's runs had been circuit clouts by big Bolavshanski. Alfie Crowell took the mound for McCloud in the top of the fourth and put the Dukes down in order. Howie was first up for the Ponies. He had bunted safely and walked, his first two times up, and now the Dukes' first and third basemen moved in close with every pitch. Howie choked up and blooped a hit over the charging third baseman's head.

Just as he crossed the initial bag, Bolavshanski put a foot out and sent him sprawling. Howie bounced to his feet and tore at the big kid, ducked under a wild swing, and brought a fist up from the ground that slammed into the first baseman's stomach. Bolavshanski grunted, and his chin came down within reach of Howie's fist. A short right hook dumped him over just as McCloud got his hand on the slack of Howie's pants.

The Dukes were too stunned to interfere, even though most of the Ponies came swarming off their bench. Bolavshanski got slowly to his feet and wiped some blood off his lips, his wide eyes disbelieving. Suddenly he jumped toward Howie, white with rage, but two of his own side grabbed him and held on. The Dukes' mentor stepped in and ordered the first baseman to the bench. "I saw you trip Patton," he said. "You're through with this team, Boly. I've warned you half a dozen times before."

"O.K. But some day I'll run into that little runt and tear him apart!" the blond giant shouted, and strode off.

Howie scored a few moments later when Willie Abendroth tripled after two were out. When he sat down on the bench near McCloud, he laughed and said, "Maybe you're right, Mr. McCloud. That guy swung hard, but I got him with the short hit."

"Watch it, Howie. There's such a thing as being too aggressive. If you feel a chip on your shoulder, knock if off right now."

"How did you get my father to let me play today?" Howie asked, as he watched Joey Brigante beat out an infield hit.

McCloud was silent for a moment. "All right, but it was worth it, wasn't it?"

The boy tried to put his feelings into words but could not come up with the right ones. "Maybe," he said under his breath. "But it doesn't give anybody the right to preach to me what's right or wrong, that's all."

McCloud chose to say nothing, chewing harder on his gum. He felt like a man caught off base by at least six feet and hoped the borrowed outboard would conk out on Harry Patton when he got in the middle of the lake this afternoon. The Ponies left the bench when Alfie Crowell flied out, and he called after them, "Hold 'em, you guys!"

The Dukes tied it up with two walks and a long single in their half of the fifth, and their little southpaw struck out three Ponies in a row in the bottom of the inning. Alfie Crowell, after walking a man in the top of the sixth, steadied down and finally got the side out, stranding two base runners. When the Ponies filled their bench, McCloud said, "Let's get a run and finish it. It's nearly noon and I'm hungry."

Ernie Colcord, the Pony third baseman, was an easy out,

second to first, and McCloud sent a pinch hitter up for Alfie Crowell, but the boy lost no time striking out. The Duke infield moved in when Howie came to the plate. Choking his bat, he looked at a pitch that nearly hit the dirt, then guessed right on one that came in too high. He swung at a curve and fouled it off. The little Duke portsider served one up he liked, and he dropped his bat and dumped the pitch down the third-base line. The Duke infielder raced in, scooped the ball up, but made no attempt to throw, for Howie was already on first.

"Go, Howie, go!" one of the few spectators shouted, and a few seconds later Howie obliged. The catcher's throw was hurried and the ball skipped out into center field when Howie slid into second. He got up and ran to third, and when the relay from the outfield was wild he kept on going to the plate with the winning run.

The Ponies pranced around him when he reached the bench, nearly tearing his shirt off. The Dukes' coach came over to shake hands with McCloud. "You've got a little jack rabbit there, Sam. My card says he stole four bases and scored half your runs."

"I hope you'll be reading about him some day, Frank," McCloud said, and then both men were hurrying toward the bus that was taking on the dispirited Dukes, for the big blond boy with the long name was striding toward the happy chattering bunch of Ponies moving toward the gate.

The Duke coach yelled, "Get back to that bus, Boly!" Three of his players moved in and backed him up.

Willie Abendroth said, shoving Howie aside, "Take two more steps, and we'll clobber you but good!"

Backing up, the big boy blurted out, "I'll be seeing you someday, you runt!"

"Sure, I hope to go to the zoo someday," Howie flung back.

Sam McCloud drove five of the Ponies home, dropping

Howie off last. As the boy got out of the sedan, he said, "You played a nice game, Howie, but I want you to remember something. Keep your chin up, not out. You lost your head so you had to use your fists, but nothing is ever settled that way."

Howie did not seem convinced, and McCloud stretched his right hand out of the car window and splayed the fingers.

"Look at the index finger, Howie. Maybe you never noticed before how crooked it is. I got into a rhubarb once and hit a man. I smashed the knuckle and never got a tight grip on a bat again. It cost me at least two years of baseball."

The boy lifted his own right hand. It had swelled up a little and was beginning to hurt. He looked at McCloud, his eyes scary.

McCloud said, with a half smile, "See you tomorrow night, Howie," and drove away, reasonably certain that the boy would never find out about the window that dropped down on his fingers in a Cincinnati hotel one night. He wished he had said one more thing to Howie, that when you make an enemy you meet him everywhere.

3

HOWIE PATTON WAS STILL SHORT OF FIVE FEET six and weighed only one hundred fifty-four pounds when he came into the gym after the game with White River that wound up the schedule in the Green Mountain League and gave Hagersville the title. During three years on his high school team he had made more hits, scored more runs, and stolen more bases than any other player of his age the native sons could remember.

McCloud must have been all wrong, the little senior thought, as he freed himself of his sweat-soaked flannels. All he had done would not be remembered as long as the home-run record established by the White River first baseman. And the homer spree was still on in the big leagues, luring the fans to the park. The old-fashioned single enjoyed the same status as the stereopticon and the bustle. Base stealing was something made popular in ancient times by men who had passed on with the Model T Ford.

McCloud drove him home. "I talked to Fred Sugden a couple of days ago, Howie," he said. "There's a job in his lumberyard for you during the summer that'll toughen you up and put weight on your bones."

"Sure, that's O.K.," Howie said, little enthused.

The sports writers gave Howie full credit for his performance in the title game but made it clear that the White River slugger had been the big gun. Two homers and a double in four at bats! It was no wonder the big kid was being offered a sizable bonus to sign with the Moguls.

"If you could grab that kind of a deal," Harry Patton told his son, "I'd say you hadn't wasted your time playing ball. Even if a bonus kid flops, he'll have the cash in the bank. Most players get kicked around in the low minors until the parent club loses them one way or another, on purpose. There's politics and personalities involved. The owners swap, sell and trade ballplayers as if they were so many head of cattle. When you've finished college, quit the game, Howie."

"I won't," Howie said, his eyes stormy.

"That job at Sugden's after graduation. Think you're big enough to handle it?"

"If it kills me!" Howie said.

It was a long summer for him. During the first few weeks at the lumberyard he was so weary at the end of the day he had nothing left for baseball, but by the end of August his muscles had become immune to the rigors of dragging heavy boards on and off the trucks. He weighed himself on the bathroom scales the night before he left for Norwich Tech and discovered he had gained six pounds. Some of that added poundage, he felt sure, must have pushed him up a little in height. He called his mother upstairs, asking her to bring the tape measure with her. In his stocking feet, he was still barely five foot six and a half. "Guess I take after your side of the family, Mom," he said, a little discouraged.

"Your Uncle Dave on my side is nearly five nine, Howie, so don't get discouraged. You still have three years in which to grow."

After a late-August workout with Sam McCloud and some local high school players, Howie was not the happiest young- ster in the world. Driving home with McCloud he reminded his friend that the fans seemed to want more and more muscle men. His kind of player was a dime a dozen. "The home-run hitters ride in Cadillacs," he said. "I'm the economy-car type."

"The little cars get you there, too," McCloud replied. "A lot of big clumsy things are being made smaller every day. Why not ballplayers, Howie?" He grinned at his passenger. "You're pretty compact and you've got eight cylinders. You've certainly got the wheels."

"You sure make a guy feel good," Howie said. "It sounds good even if it isn't so."

"I read something mighty interesting in the paper a few days ago," McCloud said, as he brought the sedan to a stop in front of the Patton home. "A couple of paragraphs about a multimillionaire named Frank Leggett. He owns three of the biggest chemical concerns in the world and is a rabid old-time baseball fan. He's willing to spend a lot of his money on what he calls a noble experiment: to restore the game of baseball to what it was in the good old days. He's building up a ball club, it seems, stressing science and speed. It is a barn-storming team on the order of an old semipro team that once played out of Brooklyn and beat a lot of major league teams."

"I wish him luck," Howie said dubiously.

"He's calling the team the Argonauts. They trained last winter at Leggett's estate in Biloxi, Mississippi. A week ago they beat the great Negro team, the Monarchs, three to one."

"Gee, they must be good!" Howie said, then shook his head and laughed. "Most likely by the time I get out of college the noble experiment will have flopped. I'd better fill up my head with electronics, just in case."

When Howie walked into the house, he fairly tasted an atmosphere of gloom. "I don't see how that outfit could put in such a bid, Grace," he heard his father say. "This is the third contract I've lost to that bunch of chiselers."

36

Howie, about to walk into the room, caught the warning in his mother's eyes and quietly made his way upstairs. His father had never confided in him as to the operations of his machine and tool company. Any rise or fall in the tide of the Patton fortunes generally reached him secondhand. A few days ago he'd overheard some men talking at the paper store who said Harry Patton was considering laying off a few men. It seemed doubtful that he would finish four years of college, at least within that number of years.

He picked a baseball up from his dresser and tossed it up and down in his hand. A small smile curled the corners of his mouth. It was round like the world and it had a cover just as hard. He hoped his future was inside it; it appeared as if it had better be.

At Norwich Tech, Howie fired up Conference baseball. On base seventy-five per cent of the time, he drove the opposition to distraction with his running. He hit short ones to all fields, seldom failed to lay down a bunt when needed, and piled up the bases on balls. The fans of the region began to take notice, and when Norwich played their archrival, Webster, over in New Hampshire, nearly a thousand came out to watch the game. They saw the sensational Norwich shortstop drive in the winning runs with his third single of the afternoon, two of which had been drag bunts he'd beaten out.

Getting out of his uniform, Howie abstractedly acknowledged the praises of his teammates, his face sober. In the pocket of his sports jacket was a letter he had received only the day before. His mother had written that his return to college in the fall was very doubtful. The Pattons faced a recession.

Once in his room, he wrote Sam McCloud a letter. Every sentence betrayed the fact that he had about agreed with his father on the subject of baseball, especially regarding a career far back in the sticks where the majority of fans were birds. He thanked Sam McCloud for the time he'd wasted on him.

McCloud's reply was in his hands just three days later, along with some newspaper clippings. It said he was still a young kid who could have the world by the tail if he'd keep his chin up and have patience. There was a man in Three Falls, New York, who was one of the backers of a Class D club known as the Saints, in the newly formed Adirondack League. Sam knew him well. He'd already phoned the man about Howie Patton, and this Joe Frazee was interested.

The Three Falls Saints are about the only outfit in that six-team league without big league affiliations, McCloud wrote, *and I'll be frank in saying that it could fold before the end of the season, but I'd grab this chance if I were you, Howie. My guess is you'll get sixty a week and expenses on the road. Knowing the ballplayer you are, it won't be long before a better club will be after you.*

Howie folded up the letter and absently tossed it aside, a bleak smile on his lips. Class D. A guy couldn't get any lower on the totem pole. He read the clippings McCloud had sent. One said that Leggett's Argonauts had beaten the major league Corsairs in an exhibition game and that owners, managers, and writers had better watch out for the brand of ball the Argonauts played. The other mentioned the fact that the barnstormers traveled in a luxurious air-conditioned bus and stayed at the best motels. Some of Leggett's players drew up to six thousand for a short season of play and came mostly from the colleges and the Class B minor leagues.

Why didn't McCloud know somebody on the Argonauts instead of Joe Frazee out in the backwoods? Well, he'd tell Frazee he wasn't interested in playing in cow pastures.

He played his last game as a collegian a week later, against Barre Teachers, and gave four hundred fans something to re-

38

member him by, getting on base four times, scoring three runs, and stealing three bases. His double down the right-field line with the bases loaded in the eighth had been the difference in the 7-5 score. He got the surprise of his young life when he reached the locker room, for Sam McCloud was waiting for him. A slat of a man, wearing a mustache, was with the ex-Little League coach and McCloud said, smiling broadly, "Howie, this is Joe Frazee of the Saints."

"Glad to know you," Howie said. He turned away and sat down to remove his spiked shoes, little impressed when Frazee told him he was even better than Sam said he was. "I'm sorry you came all the way here, Mr. Frazee," he said, and reached for words his father had often used. "I'd get kicked around, swapped, or traded in your bush league until I'm lost in the shuffle. I'd most likely break a leg stepping into a woodchuck's hole."

"Yeah," Frazee said and turned a sour smile McCloud's way. "Let's fill up the bus with gas and get going, Sam."

"Go over to the hotel, Joe," McCloud said. "I'll join you later." He waited until the other players had vacated the dressing room and then glared at the little shortstop.

Howie said, "Look, Sam! I——"

"You look! Don't turn up your nose at Class D! It's pro baseball. What do you want? To start at the top and fall flat on your face for lack of experience rather than near the bottom and let experience push you up? You've been a hot high school and college player, but that isn't enough experience in this business. Kid, your foot's in the door. Don't take it out." He turned to go. "But don't take my advice, if you're so sure you know all the answers. I won't offer you any more unless you ask for it!"

Howie took his eyes off the cement floor and looked up at Sam. "I've got a big mouth, Mr. McCloud. Tell Frazee I'll be there when he wants me."

McCloud came over to the bench and rumpled the hair

Howie had carefully combed. "You had me scared for a minute, Howie."

"I guess I just have to play ball, no matter where," Howie said.

Making a short trip home, Howie was not surprised at his father's reaction to his decision to try organized ball. He sat patiently, listening to the old harangue.

"So you've decided to be a baseball bum and end up filling gas tanks and wiping windshields! I'll tell you why, Howie. Just to show me! Hah, I'll never live that long!"

"I'm not going to quarrel with you," Howie sat flatly. He left the room.

Out in the kitchen, he took a towel down from the rack to help his mother with the dishes. Grace Patton said, "You must make allowances for your father, son. He's been having a difficult time and thinks all the world is against him. As far as I'm concerned, be a ballplayer, Howie. A good one!"

He grinned and kissed her on the cheek. "How can I miss now?" he asked.

The phone rang out in the hall, and they heard Harry Patton answer it. They heard him say, "Look, I told you I wasn't interested in peanuts. No, period, to that penny ante deal. I'm not so hard up I'll take any bones thrown my way. Thanks just the same."

Howie's mother caught the question in his eyes and answered it with a shrug of her shoulders and a deep sigh. Howie was sure he knew the answer to his father's troubles; his mother knew, too. It would make things worse if he mentioned that Harry Patton's son was also too small for him. Everybody seemed to go for the big clincher, even in business —the cleanup wallop that paid off and fast.

Howie arrived in Three Falls at noon the next day and, following instructions, took a taxi to the Central Hotel, a drab brick building adjoining a warehouse. The clerk signed him up. "Yeah, Patton. You're in thirty-one with Pete Rogell. Hope your bag ain't too heavy. This isn't the Ritz. You'll find Sayre and most of the players in the dining room."

"Patton?" a gruff voice called out. The shortstop turned and saw a heavy-set man coming toward him, a toothpick jutting from one side of his mouth. His face had a pugnacious quality which reminded Howie of a bull terrier he'd once owned. The man's eyes, his friendly grin of welcome, compensated for his nub of a nose and heavy jaw. "I'm Herb Sayre. Let's go up to my room." He kept talking as they made their way up the frayed carpeting on the stairs. "We have the makin's of a first class nut house here, Patton, but a pretty fair ball club. I know what you're thinkin'. Why am I in this bush league at my age? I'm too lazy to work and too scared to steal, kid. Ha, ha!"

When Sayre closed the door behind them, he got a long villainous cigar burning. The smoke made Howie's head swim.

"Used to smoke good ones when I played with Class AA, kid," he said apologetically. He studied his new shortstop for a long moment. "Hear you're pretty fast, Patton, a heck of a guy in a clutch. You never played night ball, Frazee tells me. Well, it's a little different, especially when you're at the plate. We play all night games except Sunday, and the lights sure ain't as bright as they are on Main Street. On the road is the rugged part, and we eat and sleep only as good as the budget allows. The bus has square wheels, hardly any brakes, and the seats have been mended with cement and baling wire. Want to go back home?"

"I'll stay," Howie said, and found Sayre's laugh contagious.

"O.K., go down there and get yourself acquainted with the other inmates," Sayre said. "Keep your hand on your watch. And Patton, I'm most likely usin' you tonight."

41

Howie made his way to room thirty-one, where he found Pete Rogell, his roommate, rubbing liniment on a sore elbow. Rogell got up and gave Howie a handclasp that made him wince; he was well over six feet and his big muscles tightened the T-shirt at his shoulders. Howie guessed he was not much older than himself. He had a tapering good-looking face, topped by a rusty crew cut.

"I banged into the fence last night," Rogell said, as Howie tossed his bag on the empty bed. He reached for the liniment again. "I play left field. The lights are murder there."

As the afternoon waned, Howie met the rest of Sayre's players, intrigued by three of them in particular, Jake Pitzer, Tom Jansky, and Sad Sid Honeycutt, the laziest looking pitcher he'd ever hoped to see. Howie wondered why this club had ever been labeled the Saints.

"One of the angels for the club is named St. Hilaire," Pitzer told him. "Haven't you jugheads briefed this kid on what he ought t' know? Twice a week we eat steak, tenderized with a special baseball bat. We ride to the ballpark at six forty-five, and if you miss the bus, Patton, you pay for a cab or walk three miles."

Howie shook his head at the floor, a grin on his face. This, he thought, was disorganized baseball.

The Saints' bandbox ball park, capable of accommodating three thousand fans, was less than half filled when the Three Falls club took the field against the Kingston Indians. There was almost an hour of daylight left. The arc lights were cold, and so were the damp hollows under Howie's arms and knees. This was the bottom rung of baseball, but the fans were just as rabid, fickle, and critical as the paying customers in the plush major league stadiums.

A few minutes later, after two of the Indians had been retired, Howie was made aware of the fact that very little money

42

was wasted on smoothing out the infield. Kingston's third hitter banged one straight at him, and he got set to take it on the short hop. The ball suddenly bounced high and went out into the outfield.

"Boo! Go back to the books, Joe College! Ya bum,ya!"

Howie's blood surged up into his neck and ears as the jeering stretched out. Louie Olmeda, the third baseman, yelled at him, "You forget eet, amigo. Ees off your chest!"

The fans got on him with a vengeance when the Kingston cleanup hitter rode the Saints' first pitch to the roof of the shoe factory outside the park. After the third out was made, Howie ran toward the Saints' bench, his eyes fixed to the ground, wishing he'd never heard of a man named Sam McCloud. Maybe his father had been right in his judgment of the game.

Herb Sayre banged him on the rear and grinned. "The best of 'em boot 'em, Patton. Field eight hundred in this league and you're a magician."

The crowd kept lambasting the new shortstop when he walked to the plate to lead off. The Kingston right-hander looked him over with maddening and disdainful curiosity. "One out!" a fan yelled. Howie ground his teeth together and choked up on the bat, trying not to listen to the merciless ribbing from the catcher, the scathing remarks from the Indians' bench. He let a low one go by, then watched a curve come in, a slow one that hung for him just right. He cut at it and drove it over the opposing shortstop's head into left center. The catcalls and the boos snapped off as he legged it to first, and then he brought the fans up and roaring when he tore for second. Kingston's left fielder, having loafed coming in to retrieve the ball, fired a strike to the keystone sack too late. Howie, grinning and dusting himself off, felt this was just about the first important hit of his life, his first one as a paid ballplayer.

4

IT WAS A RAGGED GAME, SPRINKLED WITH ER-
rors and featuring a parade of pitchers. Three Falls won in
the ninth, 9-8, when Howie beat out an infield hit, stole
second, then scored on Pete Rogell's home run over the
center-field fence. Half a hundred fans waylaid the Saints as
they emerged from their tacky dressing room under the stands.
They yelled for Rogell, clamoring for his autograph. One fan
said, as Howie passed by, "You're O.K., Patton," then followed at Rogell's heels.

Howie had to smile. He thought he'd done pretty well with
two hits and two walks in two official trips to the plate. He'd
scored three runs and stolen as many bases, but one long
bomb had discounted all of these accomplishments. Herb
Sayre, however, had given him full credit for his debut. "A
great game, Patton," he'd said, just as Howie started for the
cramped shower room. "You've sure got the makings!"

The headline on the sports page of the Three Falls *Chronicle* the next morning blared out in big type: ROGELL'S BLAST
SCALPS INDIANS. In small type the writer said the new shortstop was impressive and displayed flashing speed on the bases,
but it remained to be seen if the diminutive Patton would hit
his weight, even in Class D ball.

"Only one for five against that pitchin'," Pete griped, "but the one I got was the big one."

Howie nodded. He pictured a barnyard inside his head where some small chickens, pecking at a big fat worm, saw a big rooster come along and gobble the worm down in one big gulp. The power hitters were still picking up all the marbles in leagues big and small, despite Sam McCloud's predictions, and the men who managed to get on base to be driven in were just members of the cast. Even with his *wheels,* Howie figured the road ahead to be a long one, his destination doubtful.

Rogell sensed what was going on in the little shortstop's mind. "I'm a lucky stiff, Howie, to be born with plenty of muscle, and not born too soon. If they ever take the jack rabbit out of the ball I'll go back to driving a truck. Or if they move the fences back. The big show now is the dozen guys out to beat that alltime record for homers. One or two of them will do it yet. I dream of it. You know and I know that there are a lot of all-around ballplayers better than the big swingers. There is a chance for some guy like you to go after just as big a record: Ninety-six stolen bases! Whoever does that will eclipse the home-run hitters."

"It's silly for any man to believe he could," Howie said, but the outfielder's suggestion deeply intrigued him.

Rogell nodded. "Maybe. But look at what it would mean to the man who came closest to it. Two or three years ago, a team won the pennant with a club batting average of .249. They had the speed and they ran the big favorites ragged. This Argonaut ball club: they're proving that good little men can more than compete with good big men. You just keep hustling, kid, and don't let up."

"Thanks for the shot in the arm." Howie grinned.

"You're welcome. I felt pretty low myself when I arrived a few weeks ago." He stuffed a pipe with tobacco and grinned

45

too. "We go on the first road trip on Monday, and Herb claims it'll separate the men from the boys. And Howie, don't forget to take along some bicarbonate of soda. You're only allowed four bucks a day for meals."

The Saints dropped the second game of the brief series to the Indians and took to the road, first stop Coltonburg. Rogell had not exaggerated too much in describing the Three Falls club's bus, dubbed the Yellow Beetle. Its top speed was forty-eight miles per hour downhill, and at that velocity it came close to loosening the bridgework in the mouths of the Saints. The next ten days were nightmares of ill-kept infields, too much fried food and second class stopovers. The bus rides would have shaken up an India rubber man, Howie was certain, and all the Saints lamented the fact that the Three Falls budget could not afford the services of a traveling osteopath. They split the two games with Coltonburg and lost two out of three at Adrian, where Sayre's pitchers turned wild. Howie was hitting .298 and had stolen seven bases when the Saints moved into Groveton, but Pete Rogell's long drives were keeping the flashy shortstop's light well under the bushel.

The Groveton Redcaps were in last place and there was a firemen's carnival in town, so there were less than a thousand fans on hand when Howie stepped up to the plate to lead off for the Saints. He ran the count full, then punched a hit over the second baseman's head. With two strikes on Louie Olmeda, Howie took off for second and beat the Redcap catcher's peg by a yard, but the small crowd made very little noise. Almeda struck out and Jansky popped up. The fans came alive when Pete Rogell took his stance at the plate, and they came up yelling when the Saints' slugger backed the Redcap center fielder against the fence to pull down his bid for a home run.

The Saints broke through in the top of the fifth when Howie, with second-baseman Rocky Mutino on first, beat out a bunt for his second hit of the night. Olmeda walked, and with the bases loaded Jansky hit into a double play. Pete Rogell then hit his twelfth homer of the campaign to drive in three runs. The crowd was still buzzing when Jake Pitzer popped up to the infield. The score remained 3-0 until the seventh, when Sad Sid Honeycutt fell apart and was shelled for four big runs before Herb Sayre rushed reliefer Phil Adee to the mound. Adee stopped further damage, and in the first of the eighth Howie's speed evened up the ball game.

Rocky Mutino grounded out and Adee looked at a third strike. Howie, when he stepped in, grinned when a Groveton fan shouted, "Get that pest!" Maybe they'd started noticing him a little. He crowded the plate. The pitcher threw a fast ball high and inside that hit the visor of his protective helmet and sent it spinning off his head. Howie, shaken a bit, trotted to first. He took a long lead off the bag and drew two quick throws from the Redcaps' pitcher. He kept rattling the south-paw so Olmeda, a .251 hitter, finally walked. Tom Jansky ran the count even, two and two, and, with the base runners going, swung at the next pitch and drove it at the Redcaps' second baseman. It handcuffed the player for a moment, but he pounced on the loose ball just as Howie wheeled around third. The crowd up and roaring, the little shortstop slid into the plate just ahead of the throw.

Pete Rogell, waiting to hit, said as Howie banged the dirt off his uniform, "That don't help my RBI's none, kid."

"I figured you'd fan," Howie said, grinning, and loped to the bench.

Herb Sayre said sourly, "You didn't hear the coach at third yell for you t' stop? Next time it'll cost you ten, Patton. Pete, as hot as he is, could have drove in three."

"I was sure I'd make it, Herb."

"There's other ballplayers on this club!" the manager snapped.

Howie discreetly kept his eyes off Sayre when Pete did swing and miss for a third strike. Howie's run proved to be the difference, and in the dressing room the Saints' manager nudged Howie in the ribs in passing. "Keep runnin', kid," he said.

After the noon meal the next day, Howie and Pete found there was little a visitor could do in the town. It had no movies in the afternoon. After a walk along the river, they returned to the motel and tuned in the Mogul game, on a TV which gave the impression that the big leaguers were playing in a blizzard. The Moguls' George Trafton was circling the bases behind two runners, and the baseball announcer's voice bordered on hysteria. "Man, that was really tagged! Man, oh, man! That's number fourteen for the T-man. All the players on the bench——"

Pete turned it off and Howie thanked him. The left fielder said, "A good seven of his homers have been strictly chopsticks and rice."

"That wouldn't be sour grapes, Pete?"

Rogell grinned at his little roommate. "Could be, Howie. But that right-field foul line is a joke. I hear a couple of the big league clubs are opening schools just to teach lefties to pull the ball. And what did Trafton say the other day during an interview? The pitchers today are a lot smarter than the old ones. Hah, how many modern pitchers go nine innings and how many win twenty games? He talked through his hat."

The Saints took six of the nine road games and returned to Three Falls in second place, but a little more than a thousand fans turned out to see them open a short home stand, their opposition the Johnston Maple Leaves, enjoying first place and an affiliation with the big league Chiefs.

Reaching the bench, Sayre commented sourly, "How long can we afford a sustaining program, without a sponsor? Well, let's get the front runners, boys."

48

Pete Rogell and Jake Pitzer hit and Howie ran, and the Saints walked off with a 7-2 win. Twice the little shortstop beat out bunts and stole three bases. Twenty-four hours later, Bloomquist racked up the Maple Leaves with a four hitter, 5-0, but there was a minimum of elation in the Saints' dressing room. Only eight hundred and sixty-seven fans had watched the shutout. "They sat in their livin' rooms watchin' the big leaguers on TV," Jansky said, "with their shoes off and lots of food handy. When are the big wheels of organized ball goin' to wise up?"

Three weeks later, Rocky Mutino announced that he'd had enough; he was going back to his father's wholesale produce business and cure his ulcer. Not long after the second baseman made his departure, George Tighe, Sayre's best fireman, during a game with Kingston, walked off the mound, after he'd filled the bases on walks, and told Herb Sayre he was finished with the game. "Sue me, Herb," he snapped. "I've got my guts full of this cow pasture pool."

The Saints scraped up two new men but, harassed by rumors that they were soon to fold, went into a slump and dropped to fourth place in the league. The big blow to Howie came when the team returned from a short road trip. To keep the Saints alive, the backers of the club put through a deal. They gave Pete Rogell to the Erie Lakers, a Class B club, for two players and a bunch of cash. Watching Pete pack his things, Howie never knew a deeper feeling of discouragement. McCloud should be here right now, he thought. I'd take off his rose-colored glasses and throw them out of the window.

"Stick with it, Howie," Pete kept insisting. "Herb got himself two pretty good ballplayers, and the dough they got for me will see the Saints through until——"

"Until what?" Howie snapped back. "You tell me, Pete. I've done about everything I'm supposed to do for this bush-league outfit but grade the infield. I could stay here for five

49

years and never be heard of unless I shoot an umpire." He got up and paced the floor, savagely kicking a chair out of his path. "My father was sure right. Up to now I've netted exactly sixty dollars and eleven cents." Suddenly he went to the closet and took his bag down from a shelf.

Pete said, "Don't be a knucklehead, Howie! Give it a little more try. You're still a kid!"

Howie flung the bag on his bed, sat down, and stared at it. "O.K., Pete, but it will *be* little more, believe me!"

While Rogell emptied the dresser of his belongings, Howie sat down and wrote Sam McCloud a letter that would surely burn the old major leaguer. He told his old friend he was off his rocker if he still thought a stolen base and an old-fashioned single would ever eclipse the home-run sideshow, as McCloud called it, in the game of baseball. He'd stick it out with the Saints for another couple of weeks if the sheriff did not plaster an attachment on the ball park. Then he might try selling insurance or something.

"I'll say good-bye," Pete said, a few minutes later. "My bus leaves in an hour, and I have to make the rounds."

"Lots of luck, Pete," Howie said, a big ache in his throat. "Drop me a card sometime."

The Saints, with three new faces in the lineup, went out and dropped a 5-4 ball game to the Johnston Maple Leaves. All during the game, the fans yelled for Pete Rogell. Once, Herb Sayre just missed getting hit with a beer can when he came out in front of the dugout to motion a fielder farther back. The chant continued through the ninth. "We want Pete! We want Rogell!" They seemed to forget Howie Patton was around, although he punched out two hits, scored three runs, and stole two bases. Rogell's replacement, a husky man named Ed Kirn, had been horse-collared at the plate, and he took a blistering verbal attack from the fans as he made his way to the dressing room.

50

Peeling off, Howie found plenty of excuses for Kirn. Dropping down from Class B to this kind of league would take the heart out of any man. Howie promised himself he'd never know how it really felt. Kirn's bags were in Howie's room when the shortstop returned to the hotel. Kirn arrived three hours later, and it was more than obvious to the shortstop that the veteran had been breaking every rule in the Saints' book. He stumbled over a chair and fell against the foot of his bed. "It's O.K. here, kid," he mumbled, when Howie reached down to help him up, and almost immediately fell asleep.

Howie stared at his new roommate, imagining Kirn to be himself a few years hence. All the things his father had ever said about pro baseball began to string through his mind and make sense for the first time. He no longer felt the desire to prove his father wrong. Only a few days ago he'd read a syndicated sports column in an Albany newspaper that said millionaire Frank Leggett's Argonauts were primarily a freak team that could never compete with a big league team over a schedule of one hundred fifty-four ball games. Baseball still belonged to the long ball hitters, and four heavy bats in a lineup would prevail nine times out of ten against a bunch of banjo hitters and fast base runners. For the second time this season, the tailenders in the league had drawn capacity crowds simply because the fans wanted to watch the visiting Moguls hit the home runs.

This was a big business, Howie had to admit. Even in the Frank and Dick Merriwell books the crowd did not come out in force to see a pint-sized ballplayer run. He kept staring at Ed Kirn.

Three days later the whammy came out of a hole in the outfield, tripped Tom Jansky, and broke the center fielder's leg. Chip Santee, a player younger than Howie, took over that part of the pasture, and the Saints blew the game, 9-2, to Coltonburg.

In the dressing room, Sayre tongue-blistered his ball club. He did not exclude his shortstop. "You're doggin' it, Patton!" he bellowed. "Twice you got nailed at second, and that first time the other catcher dropped the pitch before he threw. You swung at bad pitches, and your boot in the fourth led to four runs. Maybe it's gettin' in your head you're wastin' your time here with the likes of us!"

"I had a bad night," Howie said, but he couldn't bring his eyes level with Sayre's.

"Don't insult what intelligence I've got!" the manager retorted angrily, then swung toward Ed Kirn. "You! If you're not in the sack by midnight I'll fine you fifty dollars."

Kirn said acidly, "I couldn't care less, Sayre."

There was a knock on the door. It immediately swung open and Joe Frazee came in. Howie, not even looking up, seemed to have trouble with a shoelace. But the next moment he was on his feet when Frazee said, "Herb, I want you to meet Sam McCloud. An ex-major leaguer on a slumming trip."

"Well, well," Sayre said, grinning, "I remember you, Sam. You buyin' the Saints?"

McCloud seemed not to have heard the jocose remark. He walked across the narrow room. "How are you, kid?"

There was something missing in McCloud's eyes, the shortstop knew, then hastily recalled the words he'd put in his last letter. O.K., so they were true. "Things could be worse, Mr. McCloud," he replied, a small grin around his mouth. "There could be a Class E league."

"I saw the game tonight," McCloud said. "It proved something to me, something I should have known all along. A guy gets hepped over something or somebody, and then comes a day he pulls up short and wonders why." He kept his eyes fixed on Howie while he touched off a cigar. The Saints began to empty the dressing room but Herb Sayre dropped into a chair, an expectant gleam in his eyes.

"I don't get it, Mr. McCloud," Howie said.

"Your father was right. You'll never be big enough to be a big leaguer, Howie, especially if, as you mentioned in your letter, the game doesn't change to fit your limited talents. I've led you by the hand ever since you were old enough to keep a glove from dragging on the ground. Sure, it's my fault you're in this bush league. But it'll be over in a few weeks, kid. Take my advice: go back to college. You'll meet a lot of potential insurance policy holders in the best fraternities."

"Look, Mr. McCloud," Howie blurted out, but the Hagersville Little League mentor had turned away.

"I'll take that offer of yours to stay over until tomorrow, Joe. I don't like driving at night any better than I liked playing arc-light ball."

Frazee said to Herb Sayre, "Come on, Herb, I'll drop you off at the hotel."

Howie's jaw suddenly jutted out. When the door closed behind the three men, he picked up his glove and slammed it down. "I'll show him!" he said to the wooden locker in front of him. "I'll show them all!"

The door opened. "Shake a leg, kid," Ed Kirn called out. "The bus won't wait another minute."

"It struck me, McCloud," Herb Sayre said, when Frazee's car was little more than a gill of gas away from the ballpark, "you were hurtin' worse than him."

"I didn't know it showed," McCloud said, with a small laugh, "but you're right, Sayre. You don't really believe I meant what I said to the kid? Look, I've known him since he was knee-high. He's a mixed-up, complicated little cuss. He has to have a bone to pick with somebody. First, it was his father, but he's already chewed the meat off that one and needs another. Maybe blood is thicker than water and a kid has to believe his father sometimes. I've just given him another bone, see?"

"I'm out in left field, Sam," Joe Frazee said.

"Seems there's people," McCloud continued, "who'd rather have others tell them what they can't do, not what they surely can. It fires them up. Howie Patton is a kid who wants to believe something more than he ever used to want to believe in Santa Claus, and that's 'the bigger they are the harder they fall!' when he gets to the big leagues—and you mark my word, he will—I sure hope he runs into a lot of big ones."

"Sounds nutty to me, Sam," Frazee said. "It's like sayin' a guy gains confidence in an auto race by throwing the car into reverse every other lap."

"O.K., so I didn't quite reach you, Joe." McCloud laughed. "Like those arc lights you've got. They don't quite reach to left field, either. One thing you can be sure of, the kid is going to play ball for you from now on."

"We'd better win some," Sayre ground out.

After a short silence, McCloud said, "I should have my head examined maybe for telling you this, but there's a scout from the Argonauts coming to look at Howie Patton when you play the Johnston club a week from tonight. If you ever tell the kid, I'll come after you both with a baseball bat. Let him think anything he wants to. Someday, maybe, I'll tell him about the box scores I clipped out of the papers and sent to the Argonaut manager."

"You're quite a guy, Sam," Frazee said. "It takes a lot of guts to louse yourself up with a kid I know you wish was your own, just to prove a point. I'm anything but that noble."

"No?" McCloud grinned wide. "You like the game of base-ball so much you're willing to go in the red for at least two years, Joe. How about that, Herb?"

"Suits me fine. I'd hate to go to work again," Sayre said.

54

"And I'm rootin' for Howie. Someday when he's famous, Sam, they'll write him up and maybe mention me as his first manager, who taught him most of the baseball he knows, and I'll get an offer to manage some big club and——"

"Take one of your tranquilizers, Herb," Joe Frazee said, and glanced at McCloud. "You might have gone too far, Sam, and broken that kid's heart."

"It's a chance I had to take," McCloud said. "No matter how much he thought of me, he likes baseball better."

5

HOWIE FELT MISERABLE FOR THE NEXT TWO hours. He sat in a chair and stared out into the dark outside the window of the hotel room, letting resentment against Mc-Cloud slowly build up and engulf the warm feelings he'd always had for him. The lump in his throat began to shrink and the muscles of his jaws built up. "He'll eat those words!" he said aloud, and banged a fist into the palm of his left hand. He grinned out at the dark patch of sky where a few stars twinkled. When he became a star he'd have some big letters made out of the ingredients that go into dog biscuits and he'd form them into words and make Sam McCloud eat them, one by one. The fierce grin was still around his mouth when he finally fell asleep.

The Saints arrived back at Three Falls after a short road trip that added four games to their win column and finally made the fans realize that Howie Patton was anything but a run-of-the-mill ballplayer. He had taken charge of the Saints, had them blazing. At Adrian he had stolen three bases, one a steal of home that meant the deciding run. At Groveton, in a double-header, he had been on base seven times, made five hits, and scored six runs. In the ninth inning of the night-cap, he'd scored all the way from first on a long single by Ed

Kirn, and the local paper ran a big headline on the sports page the following morning that said, "SAINTS' PATTON BEDEVILS REDCAPS. THE PEST RUNS WILD!"

Howie found a letter from home when he arrived at the Saints' hotel. His mother wrote that his father had hit the big one at last, a contract that should keep the company busy for two or three months at least. There was very little else in the way of news in the town except that Sam McCloud was heading a committee, the purpose of which was to bring Little League baseball back to Hagersville. She thought it strange that McCloud had not paid them a call for several weeks, and reminded her son that his father's bark had always been worse than his bite; if he really needed anything, all he had to do was ask.

Howie's smile was thin as he stowed the letter back into the envelope. Good old Dad had swung for the fence, too. Sometimes, however, the ball failed to clear it.

Ed Kirn's voice scattered his thoughts. "You know I'm a new man, Howie? Haven't had even a short beer for a week. You're the medicine I needed, what the whole club needed."

"Do they ever give raises here?" Howie asked. "You generally have to pay for what the doctor orders."

"Look, kid. I've got a mighty big hunch you won't be around here too long. Stay loose and happy."

The ball park was close to being full when the Saints took the field the next night against the Johnston Maple Leaves, and Herb Sayre rubbed his hands together in the manner of a miser when he reached the dugout. He fixed his eyes fondly on the spark plug, the little man out at shortstop who had at last captured the imagination of the fans around the circuit. He sincerely hoped nothing had happened to prevent the Argonaut scout from being here on this night.

Sad Sid Honeycutt threw a strike past the Maple Leaf lead-off man, and the crowd roared. The gangly right-hander hit the inside corner of the plate with a slow curve, and, after a mild protest from the hitter, struck his man out with a change-up. The next two hitters grounded out to Howie Patton, and the fans stepped up their racket when the Saints came in for their cuts. Many of them were already shouting, "Go, Patton, go!"

The Johnston infield played shallow. After Howie ran the count to one strike and three balls, he blooped a hit over the incoming third baseman's head and raced to second before the ball was thrown in. Three Falls rooters were up and howling. Louie Olmeda went down swinging but Chip Santee, Sayre's replacement for the injured Jansky, banged a single into right field, scoring Howie. Ed Kirn, hopes of returning to bigger fields burning bright within him once more, lost no time riding a fast pitch out of the park, and the stands were jumping as he scored behind Santee.

"The kid strikes the match," Kirn said, as he reached the dugout. "We touch off the kindling wood." He slapped Howie on the shoulder, then sat down and growled his impatience as Jake Pitzer and DuHamel, a newcomer, popped up.

Honeycutt stopped the opposition with no hits until the top of the fourth. Here, a Johnston power hitter reached him for a triple. A sacrifice fly followed, and the first Johnston run came in. Sad Sid burned two strikes across to the next man, then pulled the string. The hitter timed it right and lofted it into the left-field seats, and the Maple Leaves were very much back into the ball game. Sad Sid got into more trouble by walking the next batter, and Sayre waved frantically toward the bull pen. Howie trotted in to talk to Honeycutt. "The guy up there," he said; "don't give him anything higher than his knees."

Sad Sid worked too carefully and lost the hitter. The crowd squirmed when the husky Johnston catcher took his stance at the plate. He cut savagely at the first pitch and drove it to

58

Howie's right. Howie raced into the hole, dug the ball out, and flipped it off balance to second. The second baseman fired to DuHamel at first for the double play, and the crowd's noise reached far beyond the confines of the ball park.

After a rocky first inning, the Maple Leaf pitcher had steadied down. Howie got on in the Saints' half of the inning with a drag bunt that lifted the fans off their seats again, but Olmeda and Santee failed to hit the ball out of the infield. The score still stood 3-2 in favor of the Saints when Johnston's slugger hit for the circuit after two were out in the top of the ninth. Sayre picked up Willie Shafto with his eyes, when the Saints came in for the last half of the inning, and nodded him to the bat rack to hit for Honeycutt.

Shafto came through, scorching a hit off the Johnston third baseman's glove. The noise from the fans accelerated when Howie dug in to face the skinny Maple Leaf hurler. The first and third basemen charged in with every pitch. Howie bunted foul, took a called strike, then ran the count to three and two. A pitch came in he liked, and he choked up on the bat and swung. The ball arched over second and into short right, where it dropped in front of the outstretched glove of the back-pedaling Maple Leaf second baseman. Shafto ran to third on the Texas Leaguer while the fans turned hog wild.

With Olmeda up, Shafto took his lead off third. He danced around, trying to rattle the Johnston pitcher. With the count two balls and one strike, Olmeda swung and missed, and the Maple Leaf catcher rifled the ball to third and caught Shafto off. Howie tore for second and beat the desperate throw to that base, then scrambled to his feet when he saw the ball skip over the baseman's shoulder, and raced into third ahead of the Maple Leaf right fielder's throw. There was only one out, and a fly ball would bring in the deciding run. The fans, momentarily quieted by the pickoff at third, were up and screaming again.

Louis Olmeda looked out at Howie as he got dirt on his hands. His white teeth flashed. A few seconds later he hit a fly to right field, not too deep. Howie gritted his teeth, tagged up, and streaked for the plate. The ball came in a little high, and the Maple Leaf catcher had to reach up for it and then bring it down for the tag. Howie slid in under it and the umpire flashed the safe sign, then hurried for the showers. The Johnston manager chased after him, protesting violently, and half the Maple Leaf Club converged on the man in blue.

The Saints playfully roughed up the fleet shortstop as they headed for the dressing room. Herb Sayre's face wore a broad smile as he trailed along behind. If that scout had been looking on, he thought, he had been given an eyeful. The Argonauts would have to come through handsomely to get the player. He was not a bit ashamed of such selfish thoughts. After all, the Sayres liked steak on the table once in a while.

He approached the shortstop when Howie came out of the shower room. "Too bad McCloud didn't stay over, kid."

"Yeah, Herb. Sure was." Howie gave the manager a grateful smile and then turned to his locker. He eyed the slacks hanging there. The cuffs were beginning to fray, and he wondered how many more stolen bases it would take to buy a new pair. He had played in fifty-six games for this club and he had stolen thirty-nine bases. He had it all marked down inside his head. He should have a .302 batting average at the moment, and he knew he'd scored fifty-eight runs. But how far out into the outside world did the Three Falls newspaper get? He tossed his negative thinking into the locker along with an empty Coke bottle and reached for those last words from Sam McCloud. They'd see him through, he told himself, all the way.

Once in the hotel, Ed Kirn stretched out on his bed and smiled up at the ceiling. He was a happy man again; the signs of mild dissipation had gone from his rugged face. Howie

60

studied his roommate again without seeming to do so, and what he saw this time gave him plenty of heart. There was a man well in his thirties, a man who had tumbled down the ladder but was climbing up again.

Kirn said, "My pappy always said you couldn't tell where a blister would rise. They tell me there's a shortage of good pinch hitters in the majors, kid. I'll be back there someday."

"I'm not betting against it, Ed. I'm not that much of a sucker."

Kirn blew a smoke ring toward the ceiling. "Maybe we'll meet up there someday. You'll know me by my white whiskers." He laughed and came to a sitting position. "A guy should never stop dreamin', Howie. If he does, he's as good as dead."

The next day started like all other days for Howie. Breakfast, then the newspapers, a walk of about an hour along the river with Kirn and Louie Olmeda. When the ballplayers returned, the hotel clerk called to Howie and handed him a message. It said a man named Harry Webber wanted to see the shortstop in a plush motel four miles out on the highway. "He couldn't come to this crumby hotel?" Kirn asked, grinning.

Howie went up to Sayre's room and showed him the slip of paper. The manager shook his head. "Doesn't ring a bell with me, kid." he said innocently. "Come on, I'll drive you out there."

Howie remembered what Kirn had said the night before. He indulged in a sweet dream all the way to the motor court. Sayre said, when he stopped in front, "I'll wait here, kid. Don't take any wooden nickels."

Webber was a pleasant, stout man with a weatherbeaten moon face and sun-bleached bushy eyebrows. He shook hands with Howie and said, "I represent the Argonauts, Patton, and

I'll get right to the point. How would you like to play with them?"

The shortstop's heart started thumping. That would be a giant stride to where he aimed to go. "I'd like it fine," he choked out. "How did you tag me way back here in the woods, Mr. Webber?"

"We have ways, Patton. The baseball scuttlebutt reaches a long way. I liked watching you last night. Now, we want you to finish out the season with the Saints, seeing that they could take a pennant in this new Class D league, but our barnstorming schedule runs into the first week in October and you could play at least half a dozen ball games. I've wired Jim Brentwood, the manager, and Mr. Leggett that you're our man, and financial and other arrangements will be made when you join the club. I'm sure you'll like them." He consulted his watch. "Sorry I haven't time to chat, Patton, but I have an appointment with Frazee and St. Hilaire in a half hour."

"Thanks, Mr. Webber," Howie said. He wondered how McCloud was going to like this barrel of apples. He seemed to float out of the motel and into Herb Sayre's car. Before he could say anything, the manager asked him if he'd agreed to sign.

"You knew?" Howie asked.

"The scout talked to me just after breakfast," Sayre said. "I wanted you to be surprised, kid. Nice layout, that motor court. That's the kind of place the Argonauts stop at." A deep sigh escaped him. "Not many of us travel this fast, kid. Take time out sometime to count your blessings."

For the remainder of that day Howie was afraid he'd wake up any minute and find himself piling boards back at Sugden's lumberyard in Hagersville. The rosy turn of fortune scared him as well as elevating him to cloud nine, for the Argonauts were not a bunch of ordinary ballplayers. At the noon meal at the hotel the other players heartily congratulated him, and if there was a slight bit of envy in any of them they hid it well. Sad Sid Honeycutt inadvertently shook Howie up a little. "You watch it, Howie. Don't you go takin' too many chances with them wheels of yours on these lumpy infields. You just play half as good as you've been playin' and we can't lose."

Herb Sayre glared at the pitcher. "Did anybody ever tell you you had a big mouth, Sid?"

"Yeah, Herb. Leave me be while I get my big foot out of it."

Late that afternoon the Three Falls *Chronicle* was on the stands. On the front page, big black letters said: ARGONAUTS TO INK HOWIE PATTON. Shortstop to Join Barnstormers at End of Season. Deal Will Strengthen Saints, Sayre Assures Local Fans.

Alone in his room an hour before the bus took the players to the park, Howie thought of what Sid Honeycutt had said. A broken leg or ankle was always a possibility in this trade. It was a calculated risk. Broken bones healed, but more often than not they took some of the speed out of a man's legs. Who could blame him if he eased up a little the rest of the way in this league? He caught a glimpse of his face in the dresser mirror, and it quickly answered his question. Every fan in the park would. All the players, even yourself. He recalled something he'd read somewhere. "Whose bread you eat, his song you sing."

When Ed Kirn came in, Howie said, grinning, "I feel like I'm goin' to have a real good night, Ed."

It was even a better night than he anticipated. The stands were nearly full, for the Saints were only one and a half games out of first place. The home fans gave him a great round of applause when he stepped up to hit in the last half of the first

63

with the Maple Leaves ahead, 1-0. He swung at the first pitch, banged it into short left for a single, and took the extra base when the left fielder juggled the ball for a moment. Louie Olmeda fanned, and Santee hit a high fly ball to deep right, Howie taking third after the catch. The crowd came up yelling when Kirn rocked the Maple Leaf southpaw for a long double, knotting the score.

After Jake Pitzer popped up, the game turned into a pitcher's battle between the Saints' Harry Conacher and Johnston's Overman. The score was still 1-1 when the Maple Leaves came to bat in the first of the seventh. Playing in close to the grass with the visitors' pitcher leading off, Howie guessed he would not write home about his good fortune. Not quite yet. There was many a slip between the cup and the lip, as the old saw had it. He'd wait until his name was on the dotted line. He yelled, "Watch it, Louie," when Overman shortened up at the plate and bunted, and the third baseman charged in, took the ball on one short hop, and rifled it to DuHamel to get the batter by a step.

He played back for the next hitter, leaped, and caught a line drive that seemed ticketed for a sure hit, and the crowd let him hear it, long and loud. Conacher struck out the Maple Leaves' most dangerous hitter, and Howie ran in, telling the Saints to get going.

Jake Pitzer led off. After a called strike he tried to skip out of the way of a low pitch but was hit on the leg. He limped to first, where Willie Shafto took over for him. Harry Conacher, not a bad hitting pitcher, laid down a bunt that had too much carry, and Overman fielded it close to the mound, whirled, and forced Shafto at second. The crowd shouted, "Go, Patton, go!" as Howie stepped up to the plate. Twice he had reached base his first three times up. The Maple Leaf infield had to expect the bunt. Howie let the first pitch go by for a ball. He bunted the next two offerings foul, and took a look up the line at Jack Younger, coaching at third. Overman threw one low and outside but Howie wouldn't fish. The Maple Leaf infielders edged back.

Overman threw. It was a good pitch, just above Howie's knees on the outside corner. He dragged a bunt toward first not more than a foot inside the line, and the Maple Leaf catcher caught up with it first and fired in a hurry. The ball hit the dirt, skipped by the second baseman covering the bag, and rolled to the stands. Conacher piled into third, and Howie reached second standing up. Overman stared at him from the mound. "Why didn't they ship you out right away?" he called out, then turned and went back to work. He bowed his neck and struck Louie Olmeda out, and the crowd groaned. Chip Santee, however, after working the string out, hit an inside pitch on the handle of his bat and looped it over short for a single. Howie nearly ran Conacher down, scoring behind him, and the Saints were ahead 3-1.

The game ended without further scoring, Howie throwing out a pinch hitter from deep short for the last Maple Leaf out in the top of the ninth. Full-throated verbal bouquets showered the Saints as they swarmed off the field. Howie felt as big as any other man as he peeled off. It occurred to him he had only a few short weeks left in Three Falls, and he was surprised to feel a pang of regret. He'd miss this dressing room where the mop smell from the wooden floor mixed with the smell of men, steaming uniforms, and the medication Jack Younger, the coach and trainer, used on lumps and cuts. He regretted some of the gripes he'd made, but hadn't every other player rebelled at times over the bad food and the arduous road trips? McCloud could have made allowances, he thought, and his eyes grew stormy. Evidently his old mentor had caught the long ball fever. Trafton, of the New York Moguls, was filling the stands where hopeless second division teams operated. Thus far he'd poled forty-seven. A teammate, Torkl, was nearing number forty. It was a drawing card that swelled the coffers of the perennial pennant-winning team. It got more attention in most of the newspapers than the crises in Europe and the Far East.

"Sure, they want the big bang," Ed Kirn told Howie later, when they discussed the situation in the major leagues. He forced a laugh. "That's the way they say the world will end."

"It sounds like sour grapes, a little guy like me sayin' it," Howie said, "but something's happened to the game when fans will boo their pitchers for walking the Mogul sluggers and don't seem to care if the home team wins or loses."

Kirn said, "Kid, most of those fans in six or seven of those cities know they might never live long enough to see a pennant and they've got to have something to yell about. Before we ever get to the big time, I'll bet you'll see a few franchises move on to other cities." He paused and drove a heavy needle through a spike cut in one of his old baseball shoes. "If a fairy godmother rode up in a Volkswagen right now and asked what I wanted, Howie, I'd say to be a twin brother to that guy, Trafton. I would be able to afford to have these shoes fixed. Got any bicycle tape?"

The Saints beat Adrian the next afternoon, a Sunday game that drew a big crowd. Coltonburg came in on Tuesday night and Bloomquist shut them out 8-0, Howie getting three hits and two stolen bases. Sayre's club moved into first place by half a game, Johnston losing a tight one, 2-1, to the Kingston Indians. When Howie reached the hotel room, there was a letter from home waiting at the desk. They had heard of his good fortune. He surmised the Hagersville *Chronicle* had picked up the bit of sports news from one of the wire services. His father, his mother informed him, was quite relieved. He'd passed on his opinion of the move. Of course it wasn't the big leagues, but it meant he could make a half decent living, and it would be a proving ground where he could find out how far he could really go in baseball. Sam McCloud had stopped by to see the Pattons. Sam was now promoting a team of twelve- to fifteen-year-olds in Hagersville, having come to the conclu-

66

sion that the town fathers could easily be right about the pressure on the tender feelings of Little League competitors. McCloud wished Howie luck.

Howie threw the letter aside, mouth drawn tight. Sure, Mr. McCloud, you have no idea the pressure you put to bear on my tender feelings. It was fixed solidly in the little shortstop's mind that McCloud had come to the conclusion that his former protégé was unfitted temperamentally as well as physically for major league ball. As sure as death and taxes, the man would pick out a kid with muscles for his next experiment. He wished the luck McCloud had sent was a tangible thing you could return with postage. He was going to need nothing from that man, just his image kept clear in his mind.

It was Jake Pitzer who first noticed the change that had come over the little Saint shortstop. In the dressing room the following night, the veteran catcher smiled to himself. Outside there was a sprinkling of rain that was holding up the ball game. Jake knew the youngster was not conscious of his slight swagger, the trace of condescension in his voice as he spoke to the other players. Ego in callow youth, he knew, was hard to restrain. The Argonauts had sent for Howie Patton, so he had to be just a little above the rest of the crowd.

A shoe fell from Jake's fingers, and Ed Kirn said, "I don't see how you can hold even a ball of fat with those hands."

"Yeah," the catcher said, "they've been around, Kirn. For nearly eighteen years. Busted four of my fingers so far. You want to see the spike cuts on my legs?" He glanced toward Howie and grinned. The thought struck him that it would help the kid if he heard some of the grim facts of baseball life.

Harry Conacher glanced up from the old glove he was treating with evil-smelling oil. "Must feel pretty good, Howie. Not many guys your age ever——"

"It sure does. The best part of it is, I got the break on my own, Harry."

The rain came down harder and lashed the panes of the

67

two windows. Jake got up and walked toward Howie. "Patton, you don't go nowhere in this cockeyed world without help, and don't you forget it. There ain't a private little island for any man, especially in baseball. When you get into big time you're no different than a piece of real estate, and the reserve clause is a ball and chain on your leg. You might be the fastest base runner since Lincoln was president and the best punch hitter, but you can still rot on a bench and watch a clown play short because he hits a longer ball."

Herb Sayre pushed the door open and stuck his head inside. "Called off," he announced. "Go on home."

The Saints took their time getting their clothes back on. They wanted to hear more from Jake Pitzer.

Howie stared at the aging catcher.

"The scouts," Pitzer went on, all the frustrations of the past ten years sweeping in and over him, "they're ordered to go out and look for weight, pay fifty to a hundred bucks a pound for it. Crowd pleasers they want, kid, the ones who come up with the big blast. That's the drama the fans want. It's not the clever little man's game, even though he plays it the way it should be played. Oh, you'll need help, kid. And you get it anywhere you can. Baseball is big business and the muscle men like Trafton, Torkl, and the rest draw the crowds, not a flashy base runner who gets on with a ten-foot bunt."

"I've heard," Howie said, a little impatiently. "That's all I ever hear," but Pitzer's words disturbed him more than he cared to admit. There was no use mentioning certain little guys who had made a lasting impression on the fans. They'd only ask him if he thought he was half as good, and had their talents drawn twenty thousand extra fans at any one time?

Kirn said, on his way out, "I could tell you, Howie. I nearly got to the Bruins once. The deal was about made when the Minneapolis general manager remembered I'd beat out his nephew once for a berth on the Class B Ottumwa Club in the Tri-State League. I found myself traded to the Omaha Packers."

"How many of those Argonauts of Leggett's ever got to the big leagues?" Sad Sid Honeycutt asked in his lazy voice.

"Don't remember one," Pitzer replied. "I guess because, with his big bankroll, he can pay his men better than some of the major clubs do, and they can work for him during the winter or go to college. They've got a good deal and they know it." He snapped his lumpy fingers. "There *was* one guy! Name was Mitchell. The Moguls had him for a while. Hardly took him off the bench, used him for defensive purposes. He asked to be played or traded. He was traded."

Howie opened the door and ducked out into the rain, his mouth pulled taut. Pitzer grinned at Sayre. "Didn't hurt to shake him up a little, did it?"

The manager said, "The right medicine, Jake," and laughed to himself as he turned away. If the game of baseball ever returned to reasonable sanity, he mused, Howie Patton would surely be one of the reasons. He'd take bets on it. He'd give odds.

There was a ragged edge to Howie's mood when he reached the hotel. "The old guys who couldn't make it," he said to Kirn, "they should keep their gripes to themselves."

"Jake was just trying to slow you down a little bit," the outfielder said. "It doesn't hurt to hear the worst side of the game. If you find it only half as bad as he painted it—well, you will be that much ahead. There's many ways for a good player to end up nowhere. The whims of a big league crowd can make him a goat and ride him out of the league. A clubhouse lawyer, if you steal the show from him, will put the skids under you. Baseball, like the slum areas of big cities, is a jungle where you can't let up for a minute if you want to survive. Especially a hitter who swings a banjo."

69

"I'm pretty fast, though, Ed," the shortstop said sourly. "I can run away from the whole business, can't I?"

"It's a great life with the Argonauts," Kirn said. "I wish I could get some of it, Howie. No pennant scramble, no lousy politics. I wouldn't want anything more."

"I do," the shortstop said.

6

THE SAINTS WENT ON TO WIN THE ADIRONDACK
League flag by four full games. What was just as satisfying,
they finished well out of the red ink. A third reason for the
celebration that went on in the dressing room was the Saint
shortstop, who had an airplane ticket in the pocket of his
sports coat. His last plays for the Saints still ran loud and
clear in the racket of the emptying ball park, for he had made
three hits, stolen a base, and scored two runs against Coltonburg.

"I hope you aren't sore at old Jake," Pitzer said, hugging
Howie to him. "I just wanted to make sure your cap wasn't
gettin' too small for your head. Sometime you'll sneak Old
Jake into a big league stadium, kid?"

"It's a promise." Howie laughed and took another pull at
a bottle of orange pop. Tomorrow, this time, he'd be in
Topeka, and the day after that he might well be at shortstop
for the Argonauts.

"Think of us sometime, Howie," Herb Sayre said, the smoke
from his cigar seeming to sting his eyes. "Better do it often,
and you'll play your brains out to keep from ever coming
back."

"Herb, it's been good here," Howie said, choking up. He

began saying good-bye to each of the Saints. He'd be leaving early in the morning. He couldn't understand why he wasn't laughing, instead of half crying, after he'd made the rounds, but he guessed there was something in what his father had told him once. You even miss a carbuncle that has been taken off your neck if you've had it long enough.

On the plane the next morning he read a piece in a magazine about the great Ty Cobb, who had died just a few short months ago, and he clung eagerly to every printed word, especially those that gave the great player's opinion of the modern game, the powerhouse swingers that hit the long balls but struck out with disgusting regularity. At breakfast he'd read the Three Falls *Chronicle,* containing a belated box score of the latest Mogul game. With about two weeks yet to play, Trafton had fifty-two homers, Torkl, forty-nine. Attendance: 31,426.

Howie grinned to himself. The last-place Seals had drawn a little more than three thousand fans the night before when they played the Solons. The big bang was still very much the scheme of things. He sat back and wondered if his dad had scored on that big one he'd said he'd hit. He dwelt at length on the fickleness of Sam McCloud and the skepticism of veterans like Jake Pitzer and came to the conclusion that he should never forget those words of Ed Kirn's. Keep dreaming or you're dead!

Following instructions, Howie took a taxi from the Topeka airport to a motel out on the highway, a de luxe complex offering a swimming pool and restaurant. One of the longest streamlined buses Howie had ever seen was taking up most of the parking area. Gold letters, edged with blue and strung along the side of the vehicle, spelled out ARGONAUTS. He reached back for the mythology he had learned in school and grinned inwardly. It would indeed be something if he found out the name of the driver was Jason.

72

He made his way to unit 26, after making inquiry at the office, and knocked softly, the nervous thump of his heart making more sound than his knuckles. There was no answer and he turned away. Three men, heading for an adjoining unit, eyed him curiously. They were not much older than himself, Howie thought. Their young faces were lean and burned the color of freshly cured tobacco leaf. The tallest one grinned and walked toward him. "You happen to be a guy named Patton?"

Howie nodded and set his bag down. "Mr. Brentwood doesn't seem to be in."

"Like most of us," a blond Argonaut said, "Jim's having a late breakfast. Come on in our room and wait."

The players introduced themselves. Vic Riker, first baseman; Stu Ernenwine, left fielder; Larry Dru, a southpaw pitcher. Howie said he was glad to meet them all and wondered if there was another business or profession in the whole wide world where a man had to constantly adapt himself to new personalities. His eyes wandered about the big room, liking what they saw. Dru seemed to read the thoughts behind them. "Not much like Class D, Patton," he said, smiling, and the new shortstop nodded.

"It's a good deal," Ernenwine said. "We have a good bunch here, and Jim Brentwood's O.K. when you get used to him."

Dru nodded and stared at Ernenwine for a moment. "Think we should fill him in on Bolan?"

"This guy is old enough to form his own judgments, Larry," Riker snapped.

"Him also bein' a shortstop, Vic," Dru said apologetically, "I thought maybe——"

"What with, Larry?" Riker asked, a big grin widening his strong mouth. He sat back in his easy chair and seemed to be reaching for words to keep the conversation going when footsteps and voices blended just outside. One voice was pre-

73

dominant, harsh and authoritative. Dru said, "The skipper, Patton. Sounds like they didn't cook his eggs right this mornin'. Better give him at least fifteen minutes."

"Thanks," Howie said. He rubbed the palms of his hands over his knees, more jittery now than he had been during his first flight on a plane. Bolan. He wondered why that name stuck to his mind, why it should have a vaguely familiar ring. He saw no reason why it should. The most puzzling part of it was that it made him think of Sam McCloud.

The minutes ticked off. Finally, Larry Dru said, "Everything seems quiet, Patton. I'd check in."

"See you around," Ernenwine said.

Howie picked up his bag and left the room. He made a swift appraisal of Jim Brentwood as he slowly closed the door of Unit 26 behind him, feeling like a guinea pig under a microscope himself. Brentwood was a man about forty-three, he judged, not too tall but solidly constructed, without an ounce of suet. His skin was deeply weathered. Harry Webber, the scout, was with him. Webber said, offering his hand, "Welcome, Patton. You know, you look smaller than when I saw you in a monkey suit."

Brentwood said, "Big enough, Harry, the way we play it. How was the trip?" He didn't wait for an answer but kept on talking. "The terms are these, Patton: hundred dollars a game and expenses the rest of the schedule. Harry has the contract ready. We're not like organized ball, and a man owns himself if he feels dissatisfied. We only ask him to stay until we get another capable player."

"Sounds all right," Howie said. Webber took a pen from his pocket and handed it toward the shortstop.

"We're having practice this afternoon at the Topeka ball park," Brentwood went on. "You'll meet the other players. I don't have to tell you the kind of game we play; otherwise you wouldn't be here. We have three men who can hit a long

74

ball at times, but we stress speed and airtight defense, inside baseball. No publicized prima donnas."

Howie nodded. "I'm buying that, Mr. Brentwood."

The manager grinned at Webber. "Up to now the big boys in the majors aren't, kid. Harry, you tell him he's in with Iffy Oldam and Bert Kahl?"

"Number nineteen," the scout said to Howie. "I'll take you down there."

A few minutes later he was introduced to his roommates. He wondered at the thickness of the lenses in the glasses Kahl wore. Iffy Oldam laughed and said, "He's a pitcher, too, Patton. We call him Bottle Bottoms sometimes, because we figure that's what he's using to see through."

Kahl said, "I got three pair. One for dayball, another for under the lights, and a pair when the sky is overcast." He was a tall, reedy athlete, with an extra big nose and small hollows under his cheekbones, a most likable man of not more than twenty-two.

"Iffy," Howie said, as he started to unpack. "That's an odd name."

"The biggest word in the dictionary to him," Kahl said, jabbing a thumb toward Oldam, "is *if*. You'll find out."

The door swung open and Ernenwine came in with two other Argonauts. Howie swung away from the dresser when the left fielder said, "Ernie, meet the kid who is going to take your job."

Howie stared at the tall willowy man with the close-cropped flaxen hair, and the years rolled back to a day in Hagersville when he went sprawling over the first-base bag after beating out a hit. Bolan's pale blue eyes widened in recognition, then narrowed and turned cold. "Thought the name rang a bell," he said, keeping both hands in the pockets of his slacks. "Well, well, a long time, huh? Yeah, I'm Bolavshansky, but the name was too long, Patton."

75

"Water under the bridge?" Howie asked and stuck out his hand.

"Sure, why not?" Bolan said, and his right hand slowly came out of his pocket. There was reluctance in its grip; Howie knew, full well, the proverbial chicken had come home to roost. Only Bolan was a bantam rooster ready to sink his spurs.

"Old pals?" Kahl asked, when Bolan had departed. "He's not such a bad guy, when you get used to him."

"Give it to him straight, Bert," Oldam said. "He'll find out sooner or later. It's better if it's sooner."

"Crossin' him, Patton," Kahl said, "is the same as crossin' Jim Brentwood, so don't forget it. There's a story behind it. Bolan was with a Class D club in the Dakotas a couple of years back, on the same team with the manager's nephew. The bus turned over and Bolan risked his neck getting the guy out. Complete details don't matter."

"They don't," the new shortstop agreed, sourness in his voice. This was what he had been told to expect: dozens of reasons why talent was not always recognized and left to rot in the bushes; just as many reasons why journeyman ball-players made the grade. He asked in a thick voice, "Bolan must be a good player?"

"Good enough," Oldam admitted. "He can hit around .280, including a long ball here and there. Good glove man, and not too slow going up the line. . . . Webber told us you were the fastest he'd ever seen, Howie."

"I hope he's right, Iffy." Howie finished with his unpacking and slammed a drawer shut. "If Brentwood is solid at short, why did he send for me?"

"Willie Flavin jammed an ankle sliding into second last Thursday," Kahl replied. "You're insurance, Patton—utility infielder."

A voice inside Howie desperately urged him to forget the things Jake Pitzer had said back in Three Falls. Brentwood would play him. He would give him every chance.

At three in the afternoon the Argonauts went to the Topeka ball park and worked out. Brentwood put Howie at short and drove most of the hard-hit balls toward that territory. The little shortstop dug them out and cut them off until sweat came out through his flannels. Not once did his throws make Riker come off the first-base bag. Later, he took his turn in the batting cage, with the veteran Argonauts crowding close and ribbing him mercilessly. Bolan led the heckling. Once he called out, "You don't weigh a pound more than when I saw you last, shrimp! I think you've even lost a string on that banjo you swing."

Howie choked up on the bat and sprayed short hits to all fields. The anvil chorus tailed off. During a session devoted entirely to bunting, the Argonauts marveled in spite of themselves at Howie's adeptness in this department. His running had their eyes popping. His performance even tied Bolan's sharp tongue. On the bench, Harry Webber said, "McCloud wasn't kidding, Jim."

Brentwood stared out over the diamond, saying nothing. Webber said, "Play him a little tomorrow, Jim. Give him a break."

"I'll see," Brentwood said irritably. "Let me run this club, Harry."

The Topeka Jayhawks had won the pennant in their Triple A league. They had to be shown by Leggett's much-publicized barnstormers, along with the fans that turned out nearly ten thousand strong. At the end of the fourth inning, the Argonauts were trailing 2-0, by virtue of two long drives by two Jayhawk power hitters. When they trotted in for their bats in the first of the fifth, the crowd bore down on them hard. Only two of them had reached first base, thus far, off the Topeka right-hander.

Ernenwine, one of Brentwood's fastest runners, led off, and Howie, who hadn't been off the bench, joined with the others in imploring the left fielder to start things going. Ernenwine shortened up and bunted the first pitch, fouling it off. He took a ball, then another strike. He smashed the next pitch to deep short and beat the hurried throw to first by a step. With Riker at the plate, Ernenwine tore for second on the first pitch and drew a low throw from the Jayhawk catcher. The ball hit him in the shoulder and bounced out into right center. He got to his feet as if on springs and raced to third, beating the throw by an eyelash. The partisan fans' racket took on a different note. This was what they had come to see. Riker skied deep to left and Ernenwine scored easily after the catch. Babe Pierro, the center fielder and a .260 hitter with two strikes on him, got a sign from the third-base coach. With the Jayhawk third baseman playing deep, Pierro dumped a bunt up the line that stayed fair by inches and was on base before the ball could be picked up.

The Jayhawk pitcher kicked dirt up from the mound and tugged angrily at the visor of his cap as he glared over at Pierro. Iffy Oldam, batting sixth in the Argonaut lineup, was another man with fast wheels. The Topeka fielders charged in from first and third when the pitcher fired his first one, and Oldam switched his feet and blooped a ball over first that dropped fair a foot inside the line. Pierro raced to third and slid in with a second or two to spare, and now the Topeka fans were turning their needles against the home club.

Howie, regretting he was not part of the action, yelled for Tim Hardesty to keep it going, to drive Pierro and Oldam in. The second baseman ran the count full, then fouled off five pitches. A few moments later it was made plain to Howie that

78

the Argonauts banked heavily on the element of surprise and often scoffed at the hidebound rules of baseball. With only one out, Brentwood had his runners on the move with the next pitch. Hardesty cut at it and drove the ball straight at the Jayhawk second baseman, who saw he had but one play, at first. Pierro came across with the run that tied up the ball game.

The Topeka pitcher, riled, fired his first pitch into McVey, an apparent duster, and the Argonaut catcher could not get out of the way in time, the ball grazing his chest. Bert Kahl, the Argonauts' pitcher, waved his bat toward the mound, and Howie heard him say, "Throw at me and you'll get this club right at your legs, Buster!"

The jockeys on Brentwood's bench laced it into the right-hander and turned the man's neck a beet red. He missed the plate four times out of six tries, and the bases were filled. The Topeka manager came out and took the ball and waved a left-hander in.

Alex Brand, the leadoff hitter, looked toward the bench as he stepped into the batter's box. He swung at the relief man's first pitch and drilled it inside third, handcuffing the baseman for a split second. Oldam, who had come down the line with the pitch, beat the throw to the plate and put the Argonauts out in front, 3-2.

Howie, squirming with inaction, watched Ernie Bolan closely as he stepped in to hit. The guy was one of the few men on the club who hit the long ball, Ernenwine had told him that morning. Quite a ballplayer. He'd play left field, too. Bolan took a strike, let two go by that missed the corners, then hit a high pitch deep to center. Backed against the fence, the Jayhawk fielder pulled it down, and Bolan, almost to second, took off his protective helmet and fired it toward the plate.

Topeka tied it up in the seventh with a single and a triple.

The Argonauts worked a double steal in the top of the eighth but failed to score. After Kahl had retired the opposition in order in the last half, the barnstormers' first hitter was Ernie Bolan. Howie shouted encouragement, along with the others, and jumped to his feet and yelled when the big shortstop crashed a double down the left-field line. Jim Brentwood called Ernenwine back and picked up Howie with his eyes. "Get him along to third, kid. Let's see what you can do."

Howie dug in. He watched the pitch come in too high. Another missed the outside corner. The third pitch was a little wide but just high enough, and he dumped it off the end of his bat between the pitcher's mound and first base. They got him by half a step but Bolan was on third.

"Nice bunt," Brentwood said, when Howie returned to the bench. Riker came through, hitting a long fly to right, and Bolan came running home. The towhead glanced at Howie. "You slowin' up a little, Patton?"

Howie's eyes sparked. "I pushed you around, didn't I?"

Bolan nodded, the smiled coldly. "I remember you did once. Don't try it again, kid."

"What goes with those two?" Hardesty asked of no one in particular, then jumped off the bench when Pierro popped up to the Topeka catcher.

"There's never been anythin' but harmony on this club, Patton," Brentwood said to Howie. "The first guy disrupts it packs his bag and fast."

Howie glanced toward the manager, then quickly looked away, aware that he'd come to this ball club with a big strike already called against him. "I'm not a troublemaker, Brentwood," he snapped.

Ferd Whipple, a utility outfielder sitting next to him, said under his breath, "Steady, kid."

Bert Kahl, after walking the first Jayhawker in the bottom of the ninth, got the next hitter to rap into a double play. The crowd came to life when their big blaster waved his bat at the Argonaut pitcher. He rode the second pitch to deep right center, but Iffy Oldam hauled it down close to the barrier, after a long run. The victorious Argonauts ran off the field, certain they had convinced a lot of people once more that speed and finesse, bunts and old-fashioned singles could prevail against a club packed with muscle men swinging from their heels.

Howie slowly got out of his uniform, feeling as if he was but a transient here amid the talk, the ribbing, and the laughter. As soon as the injured Flavin returned to the club, Brentwood would have the excuse to turn him loose. He looked for and found Ernie Bolan. Brentwood was saying something to the player. The manager slapped Bolan on the back before he turned away. Howie caught the big guy's glance, and it said plainly that Ernie Bolan was kingpin here.

This could be one of the countless dead ends a ballplayer ran into on his way to the big leagues. Howie tried not to think of certain dread statistics. There were approximately four hundred ballplayers in the majors, and seven to nine thousand in the minors. The odds were close to twenty-five to one against him. The stinging needles of the shower and thoughts of Sam McCloud washed a lot of the despair out of him. He'd get by Bolan and run far ahead of him.

The big bus rolled south the next morning toward Memphis, where the Argonauts had a game with a great Negro team, the Monarchs. Along with most of the other players, Howie was catching up on the news, mostly the sports pages. The Moguls had stretched their lead in the younger circuit to nine games, and Trafton was close to the record of sixty homers.

Oldam, sitting alongside Howie, said, "This is something. Joe Blain, owner of the Cleveland Bulls, is sure he's had it and is considering moving the club to Oakland on the coast. Los Angeles is already bidding for a club. If there are ten

81

teams next year or the one after that means fifty more minor leaguers might get brought up. If I can hit .260 next year. If——" He swung his glance toward the paper again, read aloud. " 'Rumors are rife that a syndicate, headed by the famous Chicago restaurateur, Arnie Cashman, will see that big league baseball continues at Cleveland's municipal stadium. Cashman——' "

"That guy?" Ernenwine called out from across the aisle. "The big night club man, with a place at Vegas? Wasn't there something about his being mixed up in a basketball fix last winter?"

Bolan said, "They didn't prove anything on the guy. Isn't his dough as good as anybody's?"

"Yeah," Iffy Oldam said. "I still say they've got something inside these baseballs. I've hit a lot of line drives to the out-fields that should've dropped a long way in front of 'em, the way I swing. Now if——"

Bolan, on his way down the aisle, stopped and looked down his nose at Oldam. "If! If the hound dog hadn't stopped to scratch at a flea he would have caught the rabbit. Iffy, you swing like a busted gate. Hah, ten teams—twenty, in each big league—and most of you characters would still be ridin' this bus."

Oh, but not you, Ernie, Howie said to himself, staring out the window at the scenery flowing past. You have it made or you'll make it no matter how, using all the angles. His mind groped back to those nights when, as a Little Leaguer, he sat in his room and conjured up the wonderful and romantic world they called organized baseball. He almost wished now that it had remained a dream. So far, he had to admit, he'd found this world little better than his father told him it was.

Vic Riker had the floor. "Maybe you are so right, Ernie. I read somethin' in a magazine while I was waitin' to get a hair-cut back in Waterloo, Iowa. What George Hasler, the Mogul

82

manager, said about the likes of us: we wouldn't finish in the first division in a twelve team league with our so-called smart baseball and track men in monkey suits. Our delayed steals, bunts and fake bunts, squeeze plays and what have you, he said, would louse up a real ball club faster than a bird can gobble up a worm. We are exhibitionists."

"They forget their travelin' circus, Trafton and Torkl." Larry Dru snorted. "Without the T-men, the Moguls would be lucky to finish third. I'd sure like to pitch against those guys!"

"Maybe you will some day," Ernenwine said.

Laughter rolled the length of the bus. Bolan exclaimed, "And Riker will sing Pagliacci at the Met. How about a game of bridge?"

In Memphis, Howie rode the bench and watched the Argonauts, with Dru on the hill, play the vaunted Monarchs even through nine innings, 4-4. Ernie Bolan had booted a double-play ball in the seventh, allowing the Monarchs to tie the score. There was no scoring in the tenth or in the eleventh. Drops of rain spattered the face of pinch hitter Nick Lomski as he stepped up to open the twelfth. Lomski worked the Memphis pitcher for a walk, but Alex Brand, the leadoff man for the Argonauts, popped up to the catcher, attempting to move the base runner along.

Howie kept glancing toward Brentwood while Brand was at the plate, for the next man up would be Ernie Bolan, who was no great shakes at laying them down. The manager made no move, however, and Bolan took his cuts. He hit a three and one line shot straight at the Monarch second baseman. The big Negro pitcher flashed his big white teeth, then bore down and struck out Ernenwine. On the bench, Oulette, reserve catcher, growled, "We threw the script away!" Jim Brentwood looked at him, opened his mouth to say something, then shut it again. He got up and walked to the water cooler.

The Monarchs were sorely threatening in their half. Luman, in relief of Dru, had two men on with only one out when the rains came. They kept coming. The diamond was rapidly turning into a duck pond, and both managers agreed to call it a night.

There was a significant silence in the Argonaut's dressing room. It finally brought an outburst from Ernie Bolan. "Say it, somebody!" he shouted, as Howie tossed his almost spotless uniform into a big trunk. "I blew it! Then look out you don't lose some teeth!"

Brentwood said, "Now, slow down, Ernie. We all have bad——"

"You should have sent the rookie in there to hit for me, that's what you're thinkin'. The squirt with the fast wheels," Bolan yelled. "Go ahead and play him, Jim!"

"When I'm ready, Ernie," the manager said stiffly. "Not until then."

Bolan, headed for the showers, suddenly turned and threw Brentwood a rueful grin. "Sorry, skipper. I had to let off steam." His glance veered toward Howie Patton, and his grin faded.

Howie forgot about showering off. Anyway, he hadn't even worked up a sweat, and he wanted to get away. He was already stretched out on his bed at the motel when Bert Kahl and Iffy Oldam arrived. Oldam said, "If Brentwood had let you hit, kid——"

Howie sat up. "If, Iffy! If I didn't have rocks in my head, I'd be in a classroom learnin' how to wire up a guided missile," he said. "I don't want to talk about baseball. You mind?"

The phone rang and Kahl answered it. He handed the instrument to Howie. "For you, long distance."

His mother's voice was something he sorely needed. Was he

all right and how was he getting along? Dad—well, it seems the big one he hit would fall a little short. The bid had been just too low, and he would be lucky to break even. He would have been much better off if he'd taken several small jobs, but can you teach an old dog new tricks? One little profit at a time added up.

Howie's face was sober when he cradled the phone. Strangely enough this not so cheerful report from Hagersville gave a definite lift to his morale. A bunt, a sacrifice, a stolen base, a single added up to a run or two, along with the fashionable long ball.

"Bad news, Howie?" Kahl asked.

The shortstop smiled and shook his head. "Not exactly, Bert." He slept very soundly that night.

7

THE ARGONAUTS MOVED INTO TEXAS AND PLAYED
a strong team made up of star minor league players, and
Larry Dru gave up but six hits and won it. Howie watched
from the dugout, not daring to wonder if inactivity could take
the speed out of a man's legs and put rust in his batting eye.
In the eighth, Ernenwine crashed against the fence, grabbing
a long drive, and had to leave the game, Ferd Whipple taking
over in left field. In the dressing room later, Ernenwine could
not lift his arm, and it was evident that he was in more than a
little pain. When the bus left Amarillo, Ernenwine remained
in the hospital.

Jim Brentwood had to revise his lineup when the barnstormers faced a semipro team in New Orleans three nights
later. He put Ernie Bolan in left field and inserted the name of
H. Patton at shortstop. Bolan's eyes plainly mirrored his displeasure when the players emptied the dressing room, and
Howie was determined to play the game to the hilt when he
came out into the lights. The stands were still filling when
Alex Brand led off for the Argonauts and hit the Baton Rouge
pitcher's first offering for a single. Howie stepped in, tied up
the infield with a drag bunt, and reached first without drawing
a throw.

Ernie Bolan threw the loaded bat away, dug in, and glared

out at the mound. Howie yelled, "Get a good pitch!" Bolan looked up the line at him and spat into the dirt. He took a strike, let two go by that were called in his favor, then swung hard at a slider and popped it high to the third baseman. The crowd booed when he fired his bat halfway to the other team's bench.

Vic Riker doubled to deep right, and Howie scored all the way from first, behind Brand, his running tearing a massed gasp from thousands of throats. After Babe Pierro fanned, Iffy Oldam singled Riker home, and the Argonauts were off and running.

At the end of six complete frames the Argonauts were out in front, 8-1. Coming in from the field, Howie hoped Ernie Bolan would get hold of one. The big guy was having a miserable night, in sharp contrast to the one his replacement at short was having. Out of three at bats, Howie had reached base as many times with a bunt single, a walk, and a sharp one-baser into short center. Twice he had stolen second. Now there were fans in the seats yelling, "Let's see Patton run! Get on, Patton, and go!"

The third pitcher stopped the Argonauts until the top of the ninth. Then Bert Kahl got one of his infrequent hits. Alex Brand faked a bunt, made as if to dump the next pitch down the line, but held back in time. He swung at the next offering and flied to shallow left.

The fans were already applauding Howie Patton as he took his place in the batter's box. He chopped at the first pitch, as the infield moved in on him, and the ball arced lazily over third and hit smack on the foul line ten feet behind it. He kept running when he rounded first. The ball came on a line to the shortstop covering second, but Howie went into the bag on his stomach just ahead of the tag. On the error of omission on the part of the third baseman, Kahl raced for home but was out at the plate on a perfect throw.

The crowd was up and screaming. Howie was tearing for third even as Kahl was being tagged out. The catcher fired to the hot corner, wild, and the little Argonaut shortstop came in to score. Jim Brentwood was grinning wide when he came into the dugout.

Howie suppressed the urge to laugh and kept his eyes off Ernie Bolan. Did he imagine there was a sound nearby like steam escaping from a radiator? Why wasn't the guy out at the plate? He looked up, saw Lomski there, and caught himself almost wishing he'd strike out. But Lomski timed a change-up right and rode it into right field.

Bolan was quiet as he peeled off after the 9-1 Argonaut win. Too quiet, Howie knew. The fat was on the fire.

Jim Brentwood offered solace in a quiet voice. "You'll bounce back in a hurry, Ernie. Things always even up."

"You're not kidding, skipper," Bolan said ominously, and Howie felt misgivings churning in his stomach.

There were two more dates to be filled on the Argonaut schedule, both at home. Heading north, the players talked of the winter months ahead. There would be interviews with Leggett's personnel chief, Brentwood had told Howie, who would determine what off-season employment the Argonauts were fitted for. Most of the players, as a rule, continued with their education.

"I was always tempted to be a Joe College," Bolan said, after listening to Brand and Hardesty discussing certain campuses. "I always wanted to meet a college widow."

The corn brought hardly a trace of laughter.

Bolan, his voice edged, remarked, "O.K., I'm an uneducated jerk. Know what Dizzy Dean said once? 'Lot of people who don't say ain't ain't eatin'.'"

A few did laugh at that one. Bert Kahl, sitting with Howie, said, "You had some college, kid. Look, you could draw at least five thousand next year. Leggett would advance——"

"I want no help from anybody," Howie replied. "I'll wait until I can do it myself, Bert."

Kahl shrugged, threw Howie a grin. "I've got to admit you're no graybeard. It's your life, kid. Yeah, say you make it in this business all the way and stay up even five or six years at a salary of anywhere between fifteen and thirty thousand. You won't need a Phi Beta Kappa key."

"I'll make it, Bert. All the way."

The Monarchs came into Akron for a return engagement, and close to ten thousand fans turned out at the old minor league park. Brentwood started Harv Olrich on the mound and the Monarchs nicked him for a run. Alex Brand, starting things off for the barnstormers in the last of the first, tried to drive a pitch down the throat of an incharging first baseman but fouled out to the catcher. When Howie stepped in, the home crowd, having had advance notice of his talents, turned loose a big round of applause.

Maybe that millionaire, Leggett, is in one of the boxes, Howie thought, as he faced the Memphis southpaw. His legs felt a little rubbery and he dug his spikes in deeper, clamping the protective helmet down tighter over his cloth cap. The first throw was down the middle for a strike. The next pitch was too close in on the batter's hands. The pitcher came in with a slow curve, and Howie reached out and dumped it up the first-base line. The catcher flagged it down, fired to first, and the man in blue gave the out sign as Howie's foot hit the bag. The fans came up raging, questioning the umpire's eyesight along with his ancestry.

Ernie Bolan swung from the heels with the count even, two and two, and skied deep to left. The game turned into a hot pitcher's battle with the score still 1-0 in favor of the visitors at the end of the fifth. Olrich set the Monarch hitters down in the top of the sixth, and the crowd called for an Argonaut rally when their side came in from the field. They set up a racket again when Howie came out, swinging two bats. Howie heard Bolan say, "He can hardly carry one, that shrimp!"

Howie waited for the delivery he wanted, shortened up, and dragged a bunt past the mound, where the pitcher made a futile stab at it. The second baseman had to field it, but when he turned to throw Howie was across the bag. On first, taking a lead that had the pitcher jumpy, Howie prayed Bolan would get a hit. The sign was on, run and hit. On a two and two count, Howie took off the second the pitch was turned loose. The crack of Bolan's bat was sweet in Howie's ears. He glanced over his shoulder as the crowd came up in full cry and saw the right fielder taking the carom off the right field barrier. He rounded second, heard the warning yells from the stands as he tore around third, and put on all the speed he had in his legs. He hit the dirt and slid across home plate, eluding the backstop's tag. Banging dirt off his uniform, he jogged to the dugout savoring the delighted cheers from the Argonaut fans.

A few moments later, Ernie Bolan scored the Argonaut's second run on a long fly from Riker's bat, but there was a deadpan expression on his face when he reached the bench. He kicked Ferd Whipple's feet out of the way, when he went to rinse out his mouth, picked up a loose glove, and fired it out in front of the dugout.

The Argonauts still had their 2-1 lead when they took the field in the top of the eighth. Olrich had never been hotter. He looked down the pike at a pinch hitter, nodded at McVey's sign, and turned a fast ball loose. The batter tagged it, a line drive that seemed headed far out, but Howie leaped high and got it in the webbing of his glove, bringing a roar of amazement from the stands. Olrich grinned out at him from the mound as he fooled with the rosin bag. He went to work on the next batter and threw two quick strikes past him. He threw a curve that hung, and the batter lifted a fly ball to short left. Howie ran out with Alex Brand. The third baseman yelled,

"I've got it!" Howie was about to get out of the way when he saw Bolan come charging in. The left fielder's hundred and eighty pounds crashed into him, and the bright autumn Sunday afternoon became dark. He felt a stab of pain in his chest as he drifted down into a deep well. It caved in on him and then there was nothing.

A faint sound washed through returning consciousness, like the gentle beat of a surf on a distant shore. It resolved into the roar of thousands of people when he opened his eyes and saw the blurred countenance of Jim Brentwood. Other blobs took shape, the faces of Oldam, Hardesty, and Alex Brand.

He tried to speak but it was painful enough trying to breathe. He heard a voice that sounded like Riker's. "The bum, the no-good bum!" He remembered. Bolan had bowled him over. "Don't move him," a voice cautioned. "A doctor is coming out of the stands now."

Howie closed his eyes to keep out the glare of the sun, his lips drawn against the hurt in him. He was a little sick with fright, too, for this could mean the end of the line. He felt a cold towel on his face and opened his eyes a little. Brentwood was looking down at him. "Don't worry," the manager said. "I'm sure it's just a rib."

The shortstop closed his eyes again, a crooked smile playing at the corners of his mouth. He hated to think Ernie had done this deliberately, but all the signs were very clear.

"All right, give me room," a strange voice said, and Howie felt strong but gentle fingers reach under his shirt and explore his costal region. The voice said, "You must have bandages in the dressing room, Jim. Go get them, along with a stretcher. I'm sure this boy has two broken ribs and we can't risk puncturing a lung."

Howie heard Bolan's voice. "It was an accident, skipper. All I thought of was getting to that ball."

"Bolan," Brentwood said, loud and clear, "when you get to

91

the dressing room, pack your things and get out of the ball park. You're through, you understand? All through! Finished!"

"All right," Bolan snapped, just before Howie felt the stab of a needle, "it's a pleasure, Brentwood. I've been sick of this phony powder-puff ball club for weeks!"

Howie felt the pain drain out of him. He was sleepy. Bolan's angry voice gradually faded and became lost, along with the crowd's noise.

When he opened his eyes again, hospital smell was strong in his nose, and the events of the afternoon began parading through his mind. It still hurt a little when he took too deep a breath. He wondered how long his ribs would be strapped up. One thing he was sure of, his stomach growled for food. Voices and footsteps, muted, came in through the door that was slightly ajar. He called out, "Nurse? Hey, nurse!"

She came in, sterile skirts rustling, and the shortstop flinched a little. This nurse was nothing like the ladies of mercy he'd read about in storybooks. Her heavy-boned face bore just a trace of a smile. "You expected, perhaps, Florence Nightingale?" She asked, and whipped out a thermometer. "How do you feel?"

"Fine, only I could eat an umpire, rare."

She took his temperature. "Your dinner will be along in a minute, Mr. Patton. There's three men downstairs to see you."

"Send them up," Howie said.

"In case you're wondering, Mr. Patton, your Argonauts won the ball game," the nurse said, as she left the room.

Jim Brentwood, Iffy Oldam and Bert Kahl watched him eat his roast beef. "I went too far with that guy," the manager explained, "figurin' I had a moral responsibility, Howie. Lately I asked myself where gratitude ended. Bolan wasn't exactly dedicated to our type of baseball, not from the start. I hope I've seen the last of him."

"You never know in this game," Oldam said. "It has hundreds of paths that cross."

"You'll be turned loose in the morning," Brentwood said to Howie. "You've got an interview at two o'clock tomorrow afternoon at Mr. Leggett's main office."

Howie nodded. The nurse came in and sniffed at the air. "Whatever you're smoking, mister," she threw at Brentwood, "is worse than fallout."

"It's pure Havana," the manager said.

"Sure, from Castro's beard trimmings," the nurse quipped, and laughter filled the small room. Howie winced when his own mirth bubbled up inside him.

When the players had gone, Howie thought of Ernie Bolan. The guy would catch on somewhere, most likely with a Class B club. He hoped it would be as far away as the Mexican border or up in Saskatchewan. However, he consoled himself, lightning might strike twice in the same place but hardly ever the third time. He had to make up his mind about tomorrow, and what he'd say to Leggett's big wheel. College could wait. He wanted no money before he'd earned it.

At three o'clock the next afternoon, Howie left the offices of Chemro, Incorporated, a small cog in the Leggett public relations department. He was to report back in just seven days. He took a plane to Albany, then a bus to Hagersville, and was at his place at the Patton dinner table by seven that same day. His father's perspective had changed, he thought. But as far as baseball was concerned, Harry Patton stuck to his guns.

"You could have really been busted up," his father said. "Why don't you make up your mind this is as far as you can go in the game? They're too big and tough in the big leagues. You've got your foot in the door with a big organization that is paying you four hundred dollars a month while you're in training. Get rid of the baseball bug!"

"I've still got time," Howie insisted, "and Mr. Leggett expects me to play baseball while I——"

"Sure, public relations!" Harry Patton snorted and angrily

93

shoved his chair back. "When you break a leg he'll toss you out before you can blink an eye. The Argonauts? A traveling advertising agency for Leggett's chemical company!"

"It must pay off," Howie retorted, patience stretching thin. "Look, you're wrong about Leggett. He's got a theory about the modern game and is spending a lot of money proving it."

"I've heard the malarkey," his father snapped. "Why don't the big league scouts grab all these hitless wonders, Howie?"

"Because most of them have dough in their heads!" Howie snapped. "All they look for in a ballplayer is muscle. Who cares if he can't field or run? If he can hit the long ball between strike-outs——"

"Please, that's enough, both of you!" Grace Patton said.

"How did you finally make out with the big contract, Dad?" Howie asked, after a few moments of silence.

Harry Patton, his eyes jumping, glared at his son. "That was kind of below the belt, wasn't it?"

"I meant nothing by it," Howie said. "Believe me, Dad."

"O.K., O.K." Harry Patton forced a smile and got out of his chair. "But maybe I had it coming. I picked up a couple of small jobs today that should pay off. Let's lay down the hatchets and go into the living room."

Howie watched the opening game of the World's Series the next afternoon and saw the Moguls beat the Corsairs in a free-swinging affair, 10-8. Trafton's circuit blow won it in the eighth. There were three other homers, two by the losers, and Howie felt doubt gnawing at him when he turned the set off. He took a walk downtown and was having a malted in Gerson's drug store when Sam McCloud walked in. If he sees me, Howie told himself, he can break the ice. I won't. Then he reminded himself he was grown up, and he slid off the stool and made his way to the prescription counter where McCloud was talking to George Gerson. "Hello, Mr. McCloud," he said.

The retired ballplayer turned quickly at the sound of the

94

voice, his face breaking into a big smile of welcome. He gave Howie a rugged handshake, then seemed to quickly contain himself. "You look good, Howie. Hear you got roughed up a little."

"Sure, a little. You'd remember the guy if you saw him, Mr. McCloud. How have you been making out with the kids here?"

McCloud slowly shook his head. "They all want to kill the ball, kid. They swing from their heels, dreamin' they'll be Traftons someday." He studied the young shortstop's reaction for a long moment. "Lot of things are changin', Howie. And a lot aren't ready for it, includin' baseball, it seems. Most likely you watched that Series game today. You still think you can hit the jackpot? In a way I feel myself responsible for you, so I wish you'd take my advice. Don't bang your head against a stone wall too much longer. If your special talents aren't recognized inside a couple of years, they never will be."

"You were the one who always said I couldn't miss," Howie replied.

"Circumstances change things, Howie, even a man's opinion."

"O.K., but I won't change," the shortstop snapped. "Maybe I'll see you around before I leave." He walked out of the store.

Gerson said, "Sam, I always thought you were high on that boy?"

"Still am, George. He'll go all the way, if he's handled right," McCloud said. "That is, if people try to trip him up often enough." He eyed the druggist, little imps dancing in the corners of his eyes. "Say, George, I'll bet you can't touch your toes five straight times without bending your knees. Two dollars says you can't!"

"Too old, you mean?" the forty-nine year old druggist sputtered. "I'll take that bet, Sam McCloud."

McCloud stood by and watched the man go through the strenuous exercise.

When Gerson had won the bet, his face was reddish purple and he was breathing in painful gusts. "There, by the Lord Harry, I did it, Sam! I'd have—done it—if it—killed me!" he gasped.

"Which proves the point I just made, George," McCloud said, grinning, and put two dollars down on the counter. The druggist was still scratching his thinning scalp when McCloud was out on the sidewalk.

The winter months unwound rapidly. They found Howie, his ribs fully knitted, spending much of his time traveling, assistant to a man expert in showing films related to chemical research. The audiences were civic and service clubs. There was a real future in it, they kept telling him, but his ears were glued most of the time to the pipes from the furnaces of the hot stove league. He could hardly wait for spring when the Argonauts would go down to Biloxi, on the gulf, where Leggett owned a big estate.

In Akron he shared a small apartment with Iffy Oldam, and one night between trips, held indoors by rain, he absorbed the contents of the country's leading sporting journal from front to back cover.

Blain, in Cleveland, still insisted he would move his club to the coast if attendance continued to drop off during the coming season. The fans had soured on the Bulls. They could have a new club, if that was what they were after, from the grab bag of the League. Howie read the paragraph aloud to Iffy.

"If it only happens," Howie said, "If there's guys who want to risk their bankrolls. That's a big plant in Cleveland, and the fans have been yelling for a pennant since——"

"It says here that this guy, Arnie Cashman, is just waiting for Blain to move out of Cleveland," Howie said.

"So what?" the Argonaut right fielder asked, with a shrug

96

of his shoulders. "We aren't even in organized ball. We'd be better off if we were thirty-two-year-old fringe players."

Howie admitted it, but he reached for a phrase that never left the back of his mind. "Keep hoping, Iffy. Keep dreaming or you're dead."

"Trouble is, most of my dreams are bad," Oldam said. "I've got to stop eatin' those salami sandwiches with dill pickles before I hit the sack."

The Argonauts went to Biloxi in late April, three new names on the club roster. McVey, Pierro, and Luman had given up baseball, and three youngsters fresh out of college had stepped in to fill the gaps. They were good days on the Gulf, rich and full to Howie, and he found his jackets a little tight around the shoulders when the team broke training camp and headed home. They would have three or four days' rest and open their schedule against the Class B Elkhart club. The bus radio was on full blast, tuned in on the Bee's-Mogul game.

"Seven to one, Moguls," Stu Ernenwine said. "It is the same old blueprint. Two homers for Trafton and only the fifth."

"Shut it off!" Jim Brentwood called out from up front, and Howie felt like thanking him, for the broadcaster's voice sounded a lot like Sam McCloud's.

Bert Kahl blanked Elkhart, and then the long grind began, from town to town, from one tacky ball park to another. Howie played the game to the hilt, stealing twenty-four bases in twenty ball games, hitting .291, and running enemy battery-men out of their collective wits. And always between games he told himself what countless other hopefuls had told themselves before him. Maybe not this year, but surely the next. Forget today, tomorrow has to be better. Forget what you've heard and read.

97

In late August, Joe Blain announced to the press that he would definitely seek the commissioner's permission to move the Cleveland Bulls to Oakland next year, a move dependent upon the willingness to amend rule 1(c) governing the addition of new clubs. Not until the major league meetings in December could this be decided. Three days later, a story appeared in the papers saying that Arnie Cashman and unnamed associates were ready to put five million on the line for a new franchise in Cleveland.

The Argonauts discussed the impending radical change in the young league's scheme of things in their dressing room after losing a close one to the strong Philadelphia Hornets. Two more clubs in the league meant jobs for fifty-six ballplayers.

"Sure," Ernenwine said, as he removed his sliding pads, "and they'll come from the rosters of the other clubs in the league at seventy-five thousand bucks each. How much are we worth by the pound? Whoever pays five million for the Clevelands sure won't gamble on a bunch of barnstormers. Let's forget it and stay happy."

Howie nodded, reluctantly agreeing. He happened to glance toward Jim Brentwood, who was watching the trainer kneading the muscles of Dru's shoulder, and wondered at the Mona Lisa smile that played on his sun-beaten face.

"I wonder what players the Moguls will put in the grab bag?" Vic Riker said. "Maybe the batboy, an old coach, and a batting practice pitcher."

"Don't be bitter." Brentwood laughed. "You'd fly to them without a plane if they wanted you. There's a lot of Mogul haters, thousands in fact, who look upon that team as a machine without a soul. They're human like anybody else, with troubles, ailments, and tender feelings."

"O.K., skipper," Riker said, grinning. "But don't ask me to learn to love 'em."

98

A wild rumor boarded the Argonaut bus along with the players a few weeks later in Frankfort, Kentucky. Twenty miles out of the city, the barnstorming team was laughing it off. "Our boss might bid for the Cleveland franchise?" Iffy Oldam scoffed. "Hah, if I'll buy a piece of the Brooklyn Bridge." He sobered quickly, a deep sigh escaping him. "But if it happens? We're all dead ducks."

A scare ran through Howie Patton before he remembered the reason why Frank Leggett had gone into the business of baseball in the first place. Would a man work for years on a certain formula and then throw it away when he was sure he'd discovered the right ingredients? Big men liked to dream, too.

"Mr. Leggett has been playin' with toys," Alex Brand said. "Maybe he wants the real thing. A kid goes after a horse when he's tired of ponies."

Brentwood said, as he came down the aisle with a can of cold beverage, "Will it kill you guys to go to work?"

When the Argonauts rolled into Akron an announcement came over the radio to the effect that Leggett's office had issued a statement. There was absolutely no basis for the rumor that he was interested in a big league ball club. The newscaster said that Arnie Cashman, on the other hand, unquestionably wanted to acquire a big league club.

"Now we can relax," Jim Brentwood called out, "and think about nothing but that game with Mobile tomorrow afternoon."

Stu Ernenwine smiled and stretched in his seat like a big cat. "We eat good another year," he said.

Another year. Howie's spirits sagged. He could really move on those bases but time was faster, a thousand times faster. It could leave him flat-footed in the unlovely confine of a Class C or D dressing room.

He had one of his best days twenty-four hours later. In the bottom of the first inning he reached first on a walk, tagged up and ran to second after Ernenwine had skied to right, and made it with a belly slide that brought the crowd up roaring. After Alex Brand had struck out, he scored on a single by Vic Riker. In the third he beat out a bunt, stole second, and went to third on a fielder's choice. When the Mobile third baseman juggled Ernenwine's hard hit grounder, he tore for home and made it ahead of a desperate throw.

"Go, go, Patton!" the crowd kept chanting in the seventh, when he reached first on another base on balls. He obliged, and looked like an easy out when the catcher's throw was perfect, but he came in hard and kicked the ball out of the second baseman's glove. The infielder seemed about to lunge at Howie, and the Argonauts came out of the dugout. Howie stood his ground, jaw thrust out. The second baseman suddenly grinned. "Man, you're somethin'!" he exclaimed, then trotted back to his position.

The Argonauts won it, 4-2. That night the mills of the gods started grinding. Stu Ernenwine and Iffy Oldam came into the apartment with some grist that sent Howie's head spinning. "We stopped in at the hotel to try out the chairs," Iffy said. "We were sittin' there when who comes out of the elevators but the skipper, and if the guy with him wasn't a scout, I'll eat my favorite glove. We heard Jim say, 'Sorry, Charlie, no deal. And my word's final with Mr. Leggett.' "

"Charlie," Ernenwine said. "Could it just be the Tanager scout, Charlie Small?"

Howie's pulse quickened. Very little ever escaped him in the way of baseball news. A few days ago the Tanager shortstop had been hit by a pitch, breaking two fingers on his throwing hand, and a rookie had been brought up from a farm team. The Tanagers were only six games out of the lead in the older league.

"I'll bet they were looking at you," Iffy Oldam said. "Who else, Howie?"

100

The shortstop's lips tightened. He nudged his nose with a thumb knuckle, knowing if he orally agreed with Oldam he'd be marked as a guy with too much fatty tissue in his head. But who else could it be, seeing as how he'd done everything for the Argonauts but put new brakes on the bus. He grinned at Iffy, masking the resentment stirring under the surface. "Maybe it was you," he said. "The Tanagers want long-ball insurance."

"I'll ignore that," Iffy said, and went to the small kitchen to explore the refrigerator.

He'd draw Brentwood out, bit by bit, Howie told himself, and if what he learned added up he'd demand his right to be turned loose as a free agent.

A man nursing even a small resentment, especially an athlete, cannot perform with full efficiency. During the next two games Howie seemed to have slowed up a step, and he was thrown out three times trying to steal. He swung at too many bad pitches, and his bunt attempts backfired three times out of four. In a motel just outside of Racine, Howie was called to Brentwood's unit. "Sit down, Howie," the skipper said. "Something's eating you, and I'm sure I know what it is. You heard a scout watched us in that last home game, and you're sure he was after you. I'm not saying you're right, but I'll tell you now not one of the players on this club is expendable."

"A guy ought to be given a chance to go to the big leagues," Howie said. "How many times does he get one? When I signed the agreement last spring, I was told——"

"Sure, you could terminate it any time you wanted to," the manager said. "You can quit and make your own deal. Next year you can be fighting to get a job away from the guy they call Mr. Shortstop in the big league, an eight-year man who hits .308. Or you can take my word, and Mr. Leggett's word, that you won't regret staying with this ball club."

Howie's eyes probed Brentwood's for several seconds. What he saw in their depths was completely reassuring, and when that enigmatic smile began playing around the manager's lips, he said, "All right, skipper, I'll buy it."

He proved he had the next afternoon, when the Argonauts played a strong Wisconsin semipro team. With the score at five all in the eighth, he blooped a hit over short after Lomski, hitting for Dru, struck out. With Ernenwine up, he drew a throw from the pitcher that got by the first baseman and rolled to the wooden stands. He did not stop at second, and four thousand fans were on their feet, each one sure he'd never beat the throw across the diamond. He left his feet a good ten feet from the bag and slid in to third on his stomach, and the umpire came up with the safe sign. Ernenwine drove a fly to left, and Howie trotted in with the run that put the Argonauts ahead.

Howie was peeling off his working clothes when Brentwood came up with a lanky, bespectacled man. "This is Cy Wenzel, writer for the Milwaukee *Post,* Howie," the manager said.

The shortstop shook hands. Wenzel said, "I see why they talked about you in the Milwaukee Brewers' clubhouse a couple of days ago. You're gettin' heard from, Patton. Mind taking a little time out, after you've washed off, and giving me some of your background?"

"Sure," Howie said. There were stars in his eyes as he walked into the shower room. He'd mention his father's opposition to his becoming a pro ballplayer, and give credit to Herb Sayre. Why should he mention Sam McCloud?

8

DURING THE LAST TWO WEEKS OF THEIR SCHED-
ule, the Argonauts sensed that something hot was on the fire.
There were straws in the wind. Brentwood was called back to
Akron and did not return for four days, and when he joined
the club in Peoria he looked to his players like a cat that knew
where the fattest mouse in the world was cornered. "You've
got a few more days to wait before your sentence," he said,
smiling at some secret knowledge. "Let's go out and win this
one."

The Argonauts departed from Peoria with twelve thousand
additional miles on the big bus's speedometer and a record of
forty-two won and fourteen lost for the barnstorming season.
The big news greeted them a few hours after arriving home. It
was on the front pages of the newspapers; it came over TV and
radio. Frank Leggett was one of the bidders for the new Cleveland franchise. It was official. A substantiating story had been
released by the office of the high commissioner of baseball,
John Burridge. Howie, Oldam, and Ernenwine hurried through
their dinner and lost no time getting back to the apartment for
the seven o'clock news.

"It's true, sports fans," the telecaster said, after giving the
world news. "Frank Leggett, multimillionaire chemical king

and owner of the widely known Argonauts baseball team, wants a big league club. Leggett's bid poses pertinent questions that are no doubt already in the minds of the fans and big league managers and directors. Leggett's Argonauts have been as much as an experiment as the work going on in the Chemro laboratories, and it is no secret that Leggett has had a dim view of the kind of ball played in the majors for the past two decades.

"Carrying on his theories with a big league club is something else again. Will he bring up some of the youngsters on his semipro club? One of the players, a kid shortstop named Patton, is said to be the fastest base runner since Ty Cobb. Well, that ninety feet between sacks seems much longer in the majors.

"Arnie Cashman, the noted restaurateur and night club owner, also in contention for the Cleveland franchise, made a statement to the press early this afternoon and said he was confident Commissioner Burridge would carefully weigh all the reasons for Leggett's wanting to buy a major league club. The public likes the game as it is. It doesn't need a shot of penicillin,' Cashman said."

"I don't like the way that announcer keeps his tongue in his cheek," Oldam said, and shut the set off. "This guy, Cashman, could throw a monkey wrench. Don't forget he's a favorite of the sports and gossip columnists and picks up the tabs for ballplayers at his night clubs."

Howie remembered. Politics, personalities, all the angles. He also had read that the commissioner was elected by twelve out of the sixteen club owners and by none of the ballplayers, so he could be told how the business should be run. Unless Burridge was his own man. . . . Howie stared at the phone. Perhaps in the morning he would put a call in to the Tanagers. He'd look out for himself; he'd been doing it a long time.

Ernenwine picked up a copy of the *Sporting Times* and

settled into a chair. Oldam said, "How about a movie to-night?" but Howie shook his head, a strange feeling taking hold of him and telling him to stay where he was.

Ernenwine gasped and Howie stared at him. "Bolan," the left fielder said, "won the Saginaw League batting title with a .341 average. That's a Mogul farm club. You can't keep that boy down!"

"Maybe we'll see him again, who knows?" Howie said, and got up and walked the floor.

"What's bugging you, Howie?" Iffy asked.

"I don't know, I just don't know."

"Well, I'm goin' to see a good Western," Oldam said. "How about it, Stu?"

"Be right with you. One thing, though, no popcorn, Iffy. When you munch it you sound like a herd of hippos stomping through dry brush."

An hour after the players had gone, the phone rang. Strangely enough, Howie expected it to ring. When he answered it he heard his mother's voice. She asked how he was, then said she thought he'd want to know that Sam McCloud had had a severe heart attack that morning. His chances were no better than even.

"Gosh, I'm sorry to hear that, Mom!" Howie said. "Well, I expect to be home in about a week. I've got business to attend to first. After all, it's not like he was a relative or something."

"You do as you think best," his mother said. Her voice had become disturbingly impersonal.

When he cradled the phone he felt a quick stab of guilt, the way he'd felt the day he'd booted the double play ball with the bases full. All right, he'd call Brentwood in the morning and tell him how it was.

"You'd better go and see McCloud," the manager said, when Howie rang him up. "If you don't I'll see that you're sent down to Class D again, kid. Check with me as soon as you get back."

Howie puzzled over Brentwood's advice all the way to Hagersvile. He had to wait two days before they'd let him see Sam McCloud. When he walked into the man's room, he was shocked at the grayish hue around the patient's lips. "Howie, it's you!" McCloud said, and a pleased grin broke out on his drawn face. "They got two strikes on me, but didn't get the third one across. It looks like you're goin' to make the big show, kid."

Howie wanted to look anywhere but at McCloud. His eyes were drawn to a bulky envelope that had not been opened lying on the small table next to the bed. He caught the return address. J. Brentwood, care of the Argonauts Baseball Club, Akron, Ohio.

"O.K., Howie," McCloud said. "So I've had him send me clippings."

"Why, Mr. McCloud? You said——"

"Never mind what I said." It seemed to tire him to talk. After a few moments he went on, "I know you better than you know yourself, kid. I figured it was wiser for me to give up on you than let you do it yourself. You can't pat some men on the back, Howie. You use the needle."

"You old faker," Howie said, choking up. "But now you've thrown the needle away, what happens?"

Sam McCloud's smile was wistful. "You still have to show me, Howie, because there's a time limit. You always griped about how time could run out on you like it has on so many other ballplayers. Well, my time is borrowed. Next year, I want to have that laugh I've promised myself for a long time, the satisfaction of seeing Leggett's brand of ball turn the crowd sour on the home-run sideshow. With you in there running them ragged."

"All right," Howie said, forcing a laugh. "We'll show you,

106

Sam." He saw fatigue drawing the man's facial muscles down. "I'll stop by again. . . . Say, did you know a Charlie Small?"

McCloud grinned, his eyes closed. "I played ball with him in Cincinnati."

"Yeah, sure," Howie said. The nurse came in and said it would be better if he left. Out in the corridor, the shortstop hurried his step, lest people nearby see the tears in his eyes. That wonderful old faker had been pushing him along all the time!

The major league meetings opened in St. Louis in December. Behind-the-scenes work by Commissioner Burridge and other officials interested in the welfare of organized ball produced rapid developments. They granted the Cleveland franchise to Frank Leggett and adopted the new expansion rule. Leggett was noncommittal when besieged by the press, and their battery of questions related mostly to the new owner's disposition of the stars on the Argonauts.

"What do you think, Howie?" Oldam asked the shortstop, who had just returned from a business trip in the interests of Chemro. "He'll be taking a chance, right enough. How much big league competition——?"

"I've got a big hunch, Iffy," Howie said, grinning. "Mr. Leggett will make the experiment, at least in spring training. If we flop—well, there's always that next year."

The hot stove took on more fuel and kept crackling. Jim Brentwood announced that he had no big league ambitions and certainly would not manage the new Cleveland club. He was happy with the Argonauts and did not care for ulcers. The writers came up with three possibles: Tim Shanley, who had managed both the Cincinnati and Philly clubs; Joe Heyl, who had won a pennant for the Corsairs' Triple A club, and Ben Macklin, the veteran Cleveland coach. . . . Leggett would retain the general manager, who had never seen eye to eye with Joe Blain. . . . Arnie Cashman blasted the methods of procedure at the major league meetings and deplored unmistakable evidence of character assassination on the part of the commissioner and the officials. The fans in Cleveland, he stated, wanted a pennant-winning team, a "today's" club, not one mixed up of yesterday and tomorrow. . . . The three Mogul players likely to be dropped into the player pool were Ed Lubec, an outfielder, Wes Spinney, a second baseman, and southpaw pitcher Juan Arana. . . .

Early in January, Jim Brentwood dropped in on Howie and Iffy Oldam with news not yet released.

"This is strictly between us," the Argonaut manager said. "Macklin has signed a two-year contract to manage Cleveland." He sat back and touched off a cigar. "He's tough but fair. Seven of the Argonauts are going to camp, Howie. You, Ernenwine, Riker, Alex Brand, Bert Kahl, Larry Dru, and—" he paused, letting Iffy stew—"an outfielder named Oldam."

"Yeow!" Iffy shouted. He threw his arms around Howie and wrestled him around. "We're in the big leagues!"

"One foot in," Brentwood said, "just remember that." He waited until the words sank in and had their effect. "The front office made a deal this morning, Howie. It bought Ernie Bolan's contract from the Moguls. You'll renew old ties at the training camp."

"Oh, no!" the shortstop groaned. "Why is the whammy down on me, Jim?"

"Wheels within wheels," Brentwood said. Ned Engel, the general manager, is a brother-in-law to the manager of the club Bolan played with last season. I saw a report on Bolan, and I doubt if any player ever got a better one. Whatever we think about him doesn't matter."

Oldam snapped, "A clubhouse lawyer if I ever saw one!"

Amen, Howie said, under his breath. He looked up from the carpet at Brentwood. "Do you really think Macklin will play our kind of ball?"

108

"Leggett's paying him. Do you bite the hand that feeds you? Between the three of us, Howie, I was a little disappointed at the choice, but let's give the man a chance. Well, I'm going to miss you two, but don't you dare to come bouncing back at me or I'll throw you out fast."

"We'll sure try not to," Iffy said.

Brentwood got up to go. "The full squad is to report at Tucson, February twenty-ninth," he revealed. "Your contracts are already in the mail." He shook their hands and wished them all the luck in the book. "The writers say you'll finish about ninth in the new ten-team league, but they have rocks in their heads. There's some pretty good ballplayers off those other clubs. By the way, the new Cleveland team will no longer be known as the Bulls. They'll be the Gold Sox."

"What could be more appropriate?" Iffy asked.

"Walk downstairs with me, Howie," Brentwood said.

On the way to the street, the Argonaut manager said, "A team can do wonders with a 'take charge' guy, Howie. He sparks them up and keeps them hustling. I think you can be that guy if you play in the big league the way you played for me. You build a fire under those Gold Sox and keep feeding it."

"A rookie? Sticking his neck out like that, Jim? They'd kill me or rib me out of the park."

"Try it," Brentwood said. "You'll be surprised what happens. You want to win, don't you?"

Howie thought of Sam McCloud and the way time flew. "Yeah, maybe I will stick my neck out, Jim," he said.

A few weeks later, Howie Patton checked in at the Santa Rita Hotel in Tucson, Arizona, with Iffy Oldam. Once in their room, they exchanged grins. "This is livin', Howie," Oldam said. "If I had a pin I'd stick it into my arm to see if I was dreamin'. If I flop, I'll shoot myself."

"That bunch down in the lobby sure gave us the once-over,

Iffy. Some of the faces were familiar. I'm sure I saw Juan Arana. Wonder if Macklin's here."

They had no sooner washed off the grime of the long trip when someone rapped on the door. Howie called out, "Come on in," and Ernie Bolan obliged.

Ernie said, an uncertain smile on his lips, "Don't throw anything, Howie. The water has run under the bridge."

"And maybe dammed up somewhere," Oldam said warily.

Bolan looked taller and heavier, Howie thought, and warned himself. Even a touch of humility did not become the man, but there was an outside chance he wished to wash the slate clean and start all over. "You did a job last year," he said. "Congratulations, Ernie."

"They had humpty-dumpty pitching, kid. Mind if I sit down?"

Howie shook his head. "How many homers did you hit in the Saginaw league?"

"Twenty-four," Bolan said.

Oldam remarked, "You sure were swinging away. I was thinkin', Ernie, about——"

"Let me read your mind, Iffy. I swung away in that bush league the way the Moguls expected me to. Macklin will tell me when to and when not to, right?"

"I'd say so," Howie replied.

Bolan got up. "Well, I just wanted to set myself straight, Howie. We won't get in each other's way out there."

"Luck," Iffy said, with very little sincerity.

In the hotel dining room Howie met most of the players, including Lubec and Spinney, the ex-Moguls. There was Cass McIver and Willie Fairbrother from the Beaneaters; Ragoni, Strunk, and Havemyer, turned loose by the Bengals. Bench warmers and fringe players from every club in the younger league, the majority of them good for only two or three years more in any kind of competition.

110

Howie was halfway through his thick steak when three men stopped at the table he shared with Ernenwine, Oldam and Bert Kahl. The shortest of the trio had a squarish, big-boned face, crinkled a little at the outer corners of a pair of slate-gray eyes. His hair was sandy, but his eyebrows seemed half burned away by many suns.

"You're the kid with the wheels," he said. "I'm Ben Macklin." He picked up Howie's hand and pumped it, then introduced his companions as the two Gold Sox coaches, Turkin and Mellott. Macklin acknowledged the presence of the other three ex-Argonauts at the table, said, "See you Monday," and walked on.

"He's tough, all right," Stu Ernenwine said. "You know, Howie, I kind of wish I never got this far."

"Only about two .300 hitters in the whole draft," Iffy said, "but one thing about underdogs, they don't have too much pressure on 'em."

On Monday afternoon at the field, Ben Macklin lectured his new club and laid down rules of conduct. There would be no bed checks unless some of the players goofed and made him reach for the whip. Every man on the club could assure himself he'd get every chance to show he was a major leaguer, and he wasn't buying a ninth-place club for a minute. Not even a second-division club. "You all know the kind of baseball you're expected to play. We're going to bunt, squeeze, steal, double-steal, and run the opposition crazy. We will not try to build a team home-run record, and there'll be no swinging for the seats unless I order it. Any man who thinks he's going to build a reputation at the cost of team effort better get it out of his skull right now. All right, let's clear the dressing room."

Ten days later, Howie and the other graduates from the Argonauts, along with the minor league rookies, had to admit that in the majors the boys and the men were quickly separated. They learned things about baseball they thought they already knew. Macklin's instructions seemed endless. They were relentless, with a pounding quality felt by veteran and rookie alike. He constantly reminded them of their shortcomings, and of the brand of ball expected of the Gold Sox. The fences, forget the fences. Hit them short where the fielders "ain't." Bunt, bunt, and run, and keep running. Hit and run, run and hit. Take that extra base. The watchword is grand larceny.

Howie heard Macklin's gravelly voice while he ate, while he slept. "Patton—anticipate the type of pitch when you're leading off first. Watch the pitcher's front foot, his knee action. It'll tell you whether he's going to pitch to the batter or try to pick you off! No, Patton, you'll never hit to right that way. Here, give me that bat! . . . Kid, how many times do I have t' tell you? Hit the bag with your pivot foot makin' the double play. . . . Look, Patton, no showboat stuff. That last ball belonged to the third baseman. . . ."

The writers were out in force when the intersquad games began, risking Macklin's blistering reactions to what they'd already written about "Leggett's new baseball frontier." They admitted that the ex-Argonauts were doing surprisingly well, but could you harness up old workhorses with colts and make teams out of them? How about men like Lubec and Spinney, who had been used to taking their full cuts at the plate? There was the old adage of the futility of teaching old dogs new tricks. Macklin would be a miracle man if he proved it to be even half wrong. Howie Patton? He was living up to his advance notices, the fastest rookie they had seen for many years, but like many highly touted players before him, might even become one of those flowers that bloom only in the spring.

Coach Cy Turkin's lineup, with Howie leading off, beat Macklin's experimental first team 5-2 in a seven-inning game.

112

The rookie shortstop hoped his inner feelings were not showing as he stripped himself in the dressing room. He'd stolen two bases on McIver, the catcher turned loose from the Beaneaters, had made two hits off Danny Wade, formerly with the Detroit club. A few feet away, Ernie Bolan was griping. "That was a fat pitch I punched out in the fourth," he said, careful his words did not reach Macklin. "If I'd really swung, that ball would still be goin'."

"You drove in a run, didn't you?" Stu Ernenwine reminded the outfielder.

"Sure," Bolan said sourly. "Supposin' we'd needed three?"

Howie watched Bolan make his way to where Lubec and Spinney were peeling off. Bolan said something to the sluggers, but he couldn't make out what it was above the roar coming out of the shower room. He saw Lubec answer with a wry smile, then shrug his shoulders. At the moment he was only sure of one thing. He didn't envy Macklin his high-salaried job. A man could not be a nice guy and win pennants, and if he got too tough they'd play in anger. That would be bad, for baseball is a game of control and precision.

The grind went on, Macklin and his coaches grimly putting this hodgepodge team into something of a unit with a singleness of purpose, weeding out the hopeless ones along the way. Just before the Bruins came in from Mesa to open the exhibition schedule, Iffy Oldam received a plane ticket back to Akron. "What happened to you, Iffy?" Howie asked in a choked-up voice, as he watched the outfielder pack his bags. "You're better than you showed Macklin."

Oldam grinned. "If I just hadn't gotten so homesick, Howie. If I hadn't thought how happy I was before I came here. There's too much business to the big league game, too much pressure. I just couldn't stay loose."

"It *is* rugged, Iffy. Unless you want the majors as bad as I do, it isn't worth the money it pays."

113

"If you get time, write me a post card or somethin', Howie."

"Sure," the shortstop said, just as Stu Ernenwine, Alex Brand and Vic Riker came into the room. Oldam eyed them warily. "You get sloppy about this and I'll start swingin'," he snapped. "I'm not a bit broken-hearted. I feel like I got loose from a chain gang."

"Yeah?" Riker said, grinning. "Tell Jim I might see him soon, too. I'm hitting fifty points under Lubec."

Oldam said, "I heard something, Howie. Macklin is going to start you against the Bruins."

"I don't know, Iffy. Ollie Spicer gets a lot more dough than I do. They'll have to play him or trade him because he's that kind of a guy. I'd feel the same way."

They put Iffy Oldam into a cab bound for the airport, told him not to take any wooden rubles, and walked slowly back into the lobby of the Santa Rita. Howie spotted Ernie Bolan over in a far corner and nudged Ernenwine in the ribs. "Nice to be in the family," he said tightly. "That's the general manager with him."

9

THERE WAS NOT A VACANT SEAT IN HI CORBETT
Field when the leadoff man for the Bruins stepped up to the
plate to face Macklin's starting pitcher, Mitch Moger. The
new press box was jammed. This was the first big test, as one
sports writer phrased it, for Leggett's "Technicians" against a
club packed with power. Chicago had Hank Macy, the leading
home-run hitter in the old league, and two other swingers that
had piled up sixty round trippers between them the year
before.

When the Gold Sox filled their dugout, Ben Macklin said,
"The big boss is here, so give him a show."

Howie sat next to Mike Janosek, an infielder drafted from
Kansas City, his spikes nervously scraping the concrete, his
throat dry. On the record this was an exhibition, but it was his
first big league game just the same. He watched the Bruins take
a brief batting practice and felt deep misgivings as Hank Macy
rifled two pitches out of the playing field. Upson and Linton
followed Macy into the cage and drove hard shots against the
fences and into the seats. The cannonading kept the crowd in
an uproar.

Preliminary warmups over, the Gold Sox took the field,
Ollie Spicer at short for Macklin. Mitch Moger threw two

strikes past the Bruin leadoff man, then got him on a pop to Steckman at first. The left-hander's control was sharp, and he retired the second batter on just three pitches. The crowd stirred and began to call for the long ball when George Upson moved in. The tall Negro slugger worked the string out, then smashed a double down the right-field line, and a full-throated roar spilled out of the stands when Hank Macy stepped in. Howie found voice for the first time and shouted out at Moger, "Get him, Mitch. The bigger they are—" He suddenly quieted, remembering he was nothing here. A raw rookie heckling the great Hank Macy? Down, Howie, down, boy!

Macy fouled two pitches off, let two bad ones go by. Moger took his time on the mound before serving the slugger the next pitch. The ball scorched in, and then it was gone. Out in right Wes Spinney, converted into an outfielder by Macklin, did not move from his tracks, for all he could do was watch the ball go into orbit.

Howie looked down at his feet and shook his head, wondering how many more such blasts would begin to convince Leggett he should have stood with the Argonauts. Ernie Bolan's voice rasped along his nerves. "Man, did he rock that one!" And then Macklin was on the top step, waving to his bullpen, when Moger walked Linton. The left-hander, however, struck out the fifth Bruin hitter. It was perfectly plain to Howie and to the Gold Sox trotting in for their bats that they were not the darlings of the Tucson fans. Only a smattering of applause followed them into the dugout, and this quickly faded as the majority of the crowd evinced its antagonism for what Leggett and his Gold Sox stood for.

Macklin said, "Let's get even," when Ollie Spicer left the bat rack. Stu Ernenwine followed the leadoff man and knelt down in the batter's circle. Howie leaned forward to get a better look at Frank Challak, the Bruins' veteran right-hander, twice a twenty-game winner. He watched the man get behind

116

on Spicer, then strike him out on a fast one down the middle. Howie winced at the reception Stu Ernenwine got from the crowd and the Bruin bench. To be an ex-Argonaut, it seemed, was to be a rebel. A loud-mouthed fan shouted, "Knock him down, Frank! Stick it in the flyboy's ear!"

Challak threw two quick strikes past Ernenwine, and Howie offered up a silent prayer. He yelled out at Stu, after he'd worked the count even, "Get a good ball and drive it down his throat!"

Ernenwine dug in. He got hold of the next pitch and slashed it through the box for a single.

Challak's first pitch to Lubec was low and had to be scooped up by the Bruin catcher, and then the crowd was up as Ernenwine streaked for second. The left fielder slid in just ahead of the tag. Howie grinned wide as he caught a surprised wavering note in the crowd's racket. Ed Lubec, ducking an inside pitch, had the ball hit his bat, and it bounced out to Challak for an easy second out, but Paul Steckman hit the second pitch into short right, scoring Ernenwine. Wes Spinney flied deep to the Bruin left fielder, and when the Gold Sox took the field, most of the hecklers were reasonably quiet.

The skeptics, the blasé long-ball addicts, rose up and yelled to high heaven in the fourth when Upson hit the Bruins' second homer with no one on. Up to that point the Gold Sox had served notice that they were going to run a lot of pitchers crazy. They had worked a double steal in the third, had failed by inches to even the score on a squeeze. Howie squirmed on the bench as if a colony of termites had moved in. "Keep your shirt on, kid," Macklin kept telling him. "It's only the month of March."

The Bruins still led 3-1 when they took the field for the bottom of the seventh. Macklin nodded to Ernie Bolan when Ragoni stepped to the plate. The rookie would hit for Felipe Vila who had pitched his three innings. Ollie Spicer went to the bat rack to look the lumber over, and Howie guessed he'd get bench sores before many more days passed. A few seconds later he was off the bench, yelling when Nick Ragoni beat out an infield roller by a step.

Howie saw Bolan look up the line at Cy Turkin, coaching at third. The Saginaw slugger tugged angrily at the visor of his helmet and slammed the tip of his big bat against the plate. He missed two straight bunt attempts, then looked for the sign again. The new Bruin pitcher, Heiser, threw one in on the hands for a ball, and then Bolan swung from the heels at the next pitch and skied to short right.

Macklin called Spicer back and told Howie to get himself a bat. "Move him up, kid, and stay alive yourself."

This is what you've dreamed of doing for years, Howie said to himself as he walked to the plate. This is it, the moment of truth. His legs trembled a little as he dug in and faced the right-hander now working for Chicago, desperately trying to ignore the ruthless barrage from the Bruin bench, the catcalls and barbs from the stands. "Rabbit ears" had ruined many good ballplayers. He watched the pitcher go through his motion and held his breath. The stretch . . . the hands ready to check the runner . . . the pitch came in tight and he rocked back on his heels, the Bruin catcher laughing. The umpire called it a strike and Howie steamed inside. The next pitch was a ball.

The crowd kept jeering as he got dirt on his hands. The Bruin backstop mocked, "Goin' to throw it at Heiser and blind him, rookie?" The next pitch came in knee-high and he dumped it down the third base line, foul by inches. The Bruin infield edged in and Heiser threw a junk ball that wobbled in at half speed. Howie punched at it and looped a Texas Leaguer over first, a foot inside the line. Ragoni, a fast runner in his own right, went all the way to third, and Howie was halfway to second when the Bruin right fielder rifled his throw in. The

118

fans were up and yelling, dead sure that the runner would be cut down. Howie hit the dirt on his stomach and slid in like a greased eel, beating the throw by an eyelash.

The Bruin second baseman stared at Howie, the ball still clutched in his hand. "You're the fastest, kid," he said, with a touch of awe in his voice, then threw the ball to the mound.

Ernenwine sent the Bruin center fielder back toward the fence with a long fly ball, and Ragoni jogged in with the second run for the Gold Sox, Howie racing to third after the catch. With Lubec stepping in to hit, the Chicago infield played back, their outfield shifting toward the right, for the ex-Mogul was down in the pitchers' books as a pull hitter. Heiser fed Lubec a pitch just below the knees, and the batter promptly shortened up and bunted it up the first base line, Howie already on his way to the plate as fast as he could run. The Bruins' pitcher and first baseman converged on the ball and stopped dead, praying it would roll foul, but it came to a stop right on the line. Lubec had not even drawn a throw, and the score was even up at 3-3 as a result of the squeeze.

Settling down on the bench, Howie sensed a different timbre in the racket from the seats. A big part of the fans were getting on Heiser now, and they turned loose an angry roar when Heiser knocked Steckman down with his first pitch. They booed him to the sky when he walked off the hill after getting the Gold Sox first baseman to pop up to short.

Sal Sava, an old fireman turned loose by the Baltimore Bluejays, got in trouble in the top of the eighth, giving up a single and two walks after one man was out. Now he had Hank Macy up and an anticipatory rumble of sound built up as he looked down the pike at McIver. They began to yell for the long ball, the big kill. Howie backed out close to the outfield grass, his mouth tight, angered at that old chant, "We want a homer! Hit it all the way, Hank!"

Sava worked carefully on Macy, running out the string. One

119

of the slugger's strikes had been a long drive that had barely hooked foul. The tension built up as Sava fooled with the rosin bag, letting Macy wait. When he got set to pitch, Macy stepped out. The war of nerves dragged out when Macy fouled off Sava's next two pitches. He swung hard at the next pitch and drove it to Howie's left, a screamer that the Argonaut rookie flagged down on a quick hop and flipped to Ragoni. It was Ragoni to Steckman, and the Bruins were retired.

Spinney, first up for the Gold Sox, reached first on an error by the Chicago second baseman. One of the five dangerous speedsters in the Gold Sox lineup, he took a long lead off first, keeping Heiser rattled. With the count nothing and two on McIver, Spinney took off on the next pitch and stole second, the Bruin catcher's throw low and into the dirt. McIver struck out, but Janosek, Macklin's third baseman, worked the laboring Heiser for a base on balls. Nick Ragoni's short fly to left made the second out, and Howie moved into the batter's circle behind Lew Mintzer, an ex-Boston outfielder sent in to hit for Sava. Heiser got the word to give Mintzer an intentional pass, and when Howie Patton came up, a lot of the fans applauded.

The Bruin manager came out and strode to the mound, taking the ball from Heiser, and a chunky left-hander emerged from the visitors' bullpen, Bobo Pruett, who had saved sixteen games for Chicago the previous season. Bobo conferred with the Chicago manager and his catcher until the umpire broke it up. Howie stood by, watching the warmup pitches, feeling a touch of the shakes again. This was an old master about to go to work out there. He stepped in and matched stares with the veteran. He took a pitch that broke sharply and nicked the outside corner, let a change-up go by for a ball. Bobo threw the curve again, half speed, and Howie swung and chopped it over second for a single, scoring Spinney and Janosek, who had been running with the pitch.

Howie stood on first, basking in the complimentary roar of

120

the Tucson fans and staring over at the stands back of third where Frank Leggett sat. He thought of Sam McCloud. He must remember to send him the box score. It would do his tired heart more good than all the medicine in the world. He thought of his father who, he was sure, had seen the wisdom by now of not keeping all his eggs in one basket.

Pruett struck out Stu Ernenwine, then left the mound in disgust, throwing his glove toward the Bruin dugout when he crossed the base line. Macklin sent Larry Dru in to pitch the ninth, and the Argonaut rookie retired the side in order, getting the big slugger, Upson, on strikes. Final score: Gold Sox 5, Bruins 3.

The Gold Sox were a happy bunch in the dressing room. Howie, removing his sliding pads, looked up to see himself surrounded by writers. "You showed us something, Patton," one of them said. "You guys just might make it work for you, the old kind of ball."

"Don't ask me," Howie said. "Macklin is the manager. Me, I'm going to keep trying."

"You were great, kid," a fat scribe said. "You ran them into the ground."

"I'm not the only one," the shortstop said. "We've got seven guys on this ball club with the wheels." He heard Macklin's impatient voice.

"I'm not crowing over one exhibition game, Charlie. Sure, they looked good, all of them. I'll tell you one thing, they won't finish far down this year."

Howie explored a tender area on his right thigh and Tom Donohue, the trainer, called him over to his rubbing table. "You're goin' to give me a workout this year, Howie. You're bound to lose some skin the way you operate. Stretch out and I'll fix you up."

The sports editor of the Tucson *Advocate* waxed almost poetic in his account of the exhibition game. Coming events

121

had cast their shadows before on the sunlit diamond of Hi Corbett Field. The Gold Sox had been little Davids with sling-shots who had outshone the Goliaths with the big war clubs. Macklin's team of unpredictables had flashed speed and more speed, particularly a little greyhound named Howie Patton. "True, Leggett's Gold Sox have got a long long way to go, through the exhibition season and far into the pennant race, to prove their kind of baseball can stack up against the slower power-laden clubs," Stu Ernenwine read aloud to Howie and Larry Dru after breakfast, "and capturing the imagination of the fans with a rapier when they've screamed for the broad-sword the last quarter of a century will take some doing.

"The fact remains, however, that a consistent running game will harass the opposing pitchers and catchers, lead to wild throws and more than a few free tickets to first. The Gold Sox will bank heavily on the element of surprise, the unpredictable, and will keep opposing infields uncertain and jittery. And there are three or four men on the new Cleveland club capable of hitting the long ball if Macklin gives them the green light."

Ernenwine tossed the paper aside. "Not bad, but I don't want to read him if we start losing."

Ernie Bolan came by with Ed Lubec. "We were talking about Ed's long bunt," Bolan said laughingly. "We're wonder-in' if anybody ever hit sixty in a season and picked up fifty grand signing names to cereal and cigarettes. Last year Traf-ton made——"

"That bunt helped win a ball game," Ernenwine said. "Macy and Upson connected—but they lost."

"Sure," Bolan said, unimpressed. "Let's see if the mail's in, Ed. I expect a sugar report from a gal up in Grand Rapids."

When the rookie was out of earshot, Dru said, "I've been trying to see something in that guy I like, Howie."

The shortstop nodded. "I know what you mean, Larry." He got up from his chair when he spotted two writers entering the

122

Santa Rita. "Let's get out of here," he said, his mind not able to leave Bolan alone. The angles, the politics. He had to keep them in mind, for Bolan, he was certain, was no disciple of the long way around.

The Bruins evened things up at Mesa, winning in the tenth, 8-7, through an error by Janosek, but the writers stressed the fact that the Gold Sox had needed but five hits to fashion their seven runs. In the fourth, Howie Patton had gone from first to third on a short drive to right by Lubec. In the sixth he had stolen third base and scored on a sacrifice fly. Now they were calling them the Go-go Gold Sox.

They beat the San Francisco Hilltoppers at Phoenix, 5-1, and the Boston Beaneaters at Scotsdale, 7-3, and in four ball games they had fashioned but one homer, that by Paul Steckman. The opposition had connected for six. The scribes were sending out the word that the Gold Sox were running like crazy, getting the bases on balls, and bunting, blooping and punching out singles. They were throwing the book away, ignoring such hidebound rules as letting a fat three balls and no strikes pitch go by. Macklin had the base runners going on a pitch with only one out, calling the hit and run despite the count on the batter.

"Analyze this ball club," a dean of sports writers wrote in his column. "Macklin has five hitters that can belt them to the opposite field or any part of the field, six men they say can run the hundred in ten flat, three ex-Moguls who spent most of their last two years on the bench and never were allowed to prove their potentials. Dru and Kahl, the pitchers Leggett brought up from his crack semipro team, have fired up the pitching staff, and in Howie Patton Macklin may have the rookie of the year. This may be the ball club that will flatten the crown of the home-run derby. . . ."

Just before a two-game return series with the Boston Beaneaters, Howie picked up a letter from his mother at the hotel

123

desk. He went over to his favorite chair in the lobby and opened it quickly. Everything was fine at home and his father's business was slowly but surely improving. Sam McCloud had stopped by a few days ago, and she had been shocked by the way he had failed. He'd been warned by the doctor, he'd said, to slow down more or he would not last another year. He sent his best to Howie.

Maybe they were right about Sam, the shortstop told himself, and maybe they weren't. He was still in there swinging, with the two strikes on him, fouling them off, staying alive. Maybe until—sure, that was it, every man had one thing he believed in and wanted to come true, like man reaching the moon, like a ball club winning a pennant when given no chance at all. . . .

Stu Ernenwine's voice brought him out of his chair. The left fielder said, "Macklin is on the warpath. Have you seen Bolan?"

Howie shook his head.

"He went to Vegas yesterday with Ollie Spicer. They're not back," Ernenwine said.

The shortstop looked at his watch. "We're due at the ball park in less than an hour, Stu. We're going to find out just how tough Macklin can be."

The Gold Sox were suiting up when Bolan and Spicer came in, looking a little worse for wear. Ben Macklin's eyes flayed them before he stung them with his tongue. "You're both fined a hundred dollars!" he shouted. "You were told Vegas was off limits until I said otherwise. For a rookie you feel pretty sure of yourself, Bolan, but get it into your head you're not a fixture on this club no matter who you know in the front office. I'll talk to you alone, Ollie."

"Sure, Mr. Macklin," Spicer said.

Howie was certain the veteran was sincerely repentant. Bolan turned toward his locker, a small smile on his face,

124

and Howie asked Spicer, "The tab there must have been a big one, wasn't it?"

"It was on the house," Spicer said.

Wheels spun within wheels in Howie's head. Scraps of old hot-stove league gossip returned to his mind, along with something Jim Brentwood had said: every pennant-winning club has a take-charge guy.

That afternoon, in the last of the sixth, with the Gold Sox trailing 3-2, Howie swung at a low outside pitch for a third strike but took off for first when the ball bounced off the tip of the Boston catcher's mitt. It rolled only a few feet from the plate and the catcher's throw was good, but the little shortstop slid into the first sack an instant before the ball smacked into the baseman's glove. The Tucson crowd, pro-Gold Sox now, yelled for Howie to go.

Stu Ernenwine bunted. The Beaneater pitcher pounced on it a few feet from the right of the mound and elected to fire to second, where he failed to get the Gold Sox shortstop by a foot. Lubec checked with Cy Turkin for the sign, then grinned wide when he dug in at the plate. Howie knew that he'd been given a green light. The ex-Mogul outfielder, swinging for the fences, struck out, and he threw his bat halfway to the dugout.

With one out, Howie watched the Boston pitcher closely. He knew after two pitches to Steckman that he was trying to keep the ball low. The count even at one and one, the right-hander fired one low and outside which the catcher had to lunge for, and Howie poured on the coal and tore for third. The throw to the hot corner was high and the third baseman had to leap to pull it down. While Howie slid in Ernenwine was less than ten feet from second base. He drew a throw but plowed in ahead of the tag. The fans were off their seats and yelling their lungs out, and Howie, taking his lead off third,

125

knew they wouldn't have made more noise if they'd seen a home run with the bases full.

Steckman popped up to the Boston catcher, but the crowd was up and roaring once more when Wes Spinney hit a one and two pitch into center to score Howie and Ernenwine. The Gold Sox had scored two runs on one hit and had gone out ahead, 4-3.

Larry Dru came in to pitch the last three innings and allowed but one hit, and the Gold Sox ran to the dressing room with a 6-3 victory, most of them managing to escape the clutching hands of the fans spilling out over the field. Spinney, who had hit a ball out of the park in the eighth, grinned at Macklin. "You going to fire me?"

Macklin laughed. "The recipe calls for a little of everything, Wes, not too much of one thing."

Dru said sheepishly, as they congratulated him, "They were taking toeholds. I got four of them on bad pitches, Ben."

"You'll get a lot more swingers that way," McIver said, and glanced at Howie. "That kid is going to cost Leggett. With the mileage he makes, how often will he need retreads?"

Howie's laugh was short-lived. He was looking at Bolan and Lubec.

10

THE GOLD SOX, EIGHT MEN CUT FROM THE roster, broke camp at Tucson the last week in March and barnstormed toward home, playing top minor league clubs en route. Macklin, little concerned with a pre-season won-and-lost record, used unseasoned players for the most part, saving his "wheels" for the torrid days ahead when the chips would be down. Howie, the times he rode the bench, watched Ollie Spicer play short. He felt a kind of sadness, for it was plain that Ollie's best years were behind him. He had never hit over .260. Looking out at Bolan when the rookie played left field, he wondered why Harry Turcott, up from Topeka, had been cut loose, for Ernie's play this spring had been unimpressive.

In the dressing room at Covington, Kentucky, waiting out a rain squall, Ben Macklin parried thrusts from the writers. "I know, Dan," he said to one. "I read what the manager of the Moguls said yesterday. We're a bunch of freaks with a certain amount of momentum that might carry us along in the first division for a few weeks, and then the law of averages plus Mogul power will put us in our rightful places. Let me tell you something, all of you guys: this is a team that won't fall over and play dead when those guys appear on the field. You quote me."

"Sure, Ben, it'll be a pleasure," a Chicago writer said. "The fans in Cleveland figured the old club did just that!"

"How about you, Howie?" a Cleveland scribe asked. "Think you can run on those Mogul catchers?"

"I'll be trying!" Howie snapped.

"You won only three of your last six against minor league opposition," another scribe said, tongue in cheek.

Macklin grinned. "That's right, isn't it? We've sure slowed down, my friend. I doubt if we can beat the Colts tonight."

The game got underway a half hour late. Macklin sent Bert Kahl in to pitch. He had Vic Riker playing first base, and Alex Brand at second. Fidel Cortena, up from the Washington Solons, was at third in place of Janosek. Rain had given the skin part of the infield a burnt umber color, and the outfield grass was soggy.

From the outset the Colt rooters poured it on the Gold Sox, reminding them that Covington was a Mogul farm club. They reveled in the error Ernenwine made in the top of the second when he slipped in the mud trying for a line drive, and jeered in the fourth when Alex Brand lost the handle on a sure double-play ball. Going into the seventh, the Gold Sox trailed, 4-1, although Bert Kahl had given up but four hits.

Ernie Bolan could not stay quiet on the bench, and Lubec, Spinney and Steckman were muttering under their breaths. Macklin ignored them, if he heard, and just stared out at the action as if it were only on tape and coming through his TV set. His expression did not change when Cortena made the third out in the top of the ninth by striking out, leaving the tieing runs on the bases. It was the Colts' game, 4-2.

In the visitors' dressing room, Ernie Bolan threw a spiked shoe against the locker. "How lousy can we get?" he shouted. "The Moguls beat that bunch, 14-1."

"Knock it off," Macklin said. "It suits me fine that we looked bad tonight. I'd sure like to see the report the Mogul scouts turn in to the New York front office!"

128

"You!" Bolan said, with a trace of sarcasm, "a psychologist?"

"You, Bolan!" Macklin threw back, "a clutch hitter? I'll warn you for the last time. I've got no time for clubhouse lawyers!"

Howie lowered his head to hide a grin, but it quickly faded from his lips. There were no writers in here, but there was that superstition about walls having ears, and he would not be a bit surprised if tomorrow's sports pages carried the news that dissension had already raised its ugly head in the camp of the Gold Sox, that one warring faction led by the ex-Mogul draftees were demanding powerhouse ball. Slowly getting into his street clothes, the little shortstop suddenly thought of Arnie Cashman and wondered why, and then his mind turned to Sam McCloud who had built him from a little leaguer to the status he enjoyed now, a man who could not be sure of a next year. Leaving the dressing room, he said to himself, "Sam, I guess I will have to take charge."

During the next few days the top sports writers offered but mild conjectures as to the singleness of purpose in a team expected to conform to Leggett's pattern of play. One quoted George Hasler, the Mogul manager. "The public still wants the long ball, and there are players on Leggett's club that know the value of it, especially when a new spring comes around and they look at the figures on their contracts. There have been other so-called go-go teams in baseball that ran themselves out early in the race. We'd say that Ben Macklin has the toughest assignment in both leagues."

Two days before the opener with the Bengals in Detroit, Howie and Stu Ernenwine rented a small apartment in Cleveland Heights, being careful not to sign too long a lease, for that morning the Cleveland sports experts had predicted the final standing of the American League clubs come October first:

129

NEW YORK

DETROIT

BALTIMORE

OAKLAND

CHICAGO

MINNESOTA

WASHINGTON

CLEVELAND

BOSTON

KANSAS CITY

The jitters were beginning to have their way with the short-stop. He could not relax—kept moving around. "You know, Stu," he said, "I've never been in a big league ball park. That stadium holds nearly sixty thousand people. Imagine them all yelling at a guy up at bat?"

"Don't remind me," Ernenwine said. "I'm even hoping Macklin starts Lew Mintzer in left. Another thing, I hate fly-ing, Howie."

"Detroit is tough. They ran second to the Moguls last year," Howie said, pacing up and down. "They're going to start that left-hander against us, Dario Masi. It'll be for blood here on in." He grinned at Ernenwine. "You'll start because Mintzer hits from the left side, and so does Janosek. Alex Brand most likely will be at third."

The hours seemed to fly and then the Gold Sox were in the dressing room at the stadium, pulling on the gray road flan-nels, the golden socks. From outside came the steady, muffled roar of the big opening-day crowd. The veterans took it calmly, occasionally taking time out to reassure the rookies, who plainly betrayed the signs of stage fright. Wes Spinney moved toward Howie, who was taking a long time lacing his spikes. "It's just another ball game, kid. Keep running, keep punching that ball."

130

Ernie Bolan shouted from the other end of the room, "He's nervous, Wes? Maybe that crowd will like banjo music mixed with that bazooka Frank Knorr takes to the plate."

Lubec and Steckman laughed a little, but Howie saw Macklin's sharp eye blaze for a moment. "You are a riot, Bolan!" he said acidly. He glanced around to see if any writers had sneaked in, then announced he had something to say and that everybody listen carefully.

"I want to make one thing plain," Macklin began. "This is a race for a pennant, for survival for a lot of you. Bear in mind every minute that all the guys you play against are out to rob you of your bread and butter. One thing I've seen the past couple of years that makes me sick at my stomach is players laughing and kidding with the opposition when they're up at bat or on base and six or seven runs behind. I'll fine any man on this ball club twenty-five dollars if I catch him doing that. If you meet them on the street I don't care if you kiss 'em, but during a ball game you let them know they're just so many men, enemies with so many faces, that you'll knock them over if they get in your way. This isn't a college campus, it's cold-blooded business where your salaries depend on how you produce, and a Series check runs into thousands. I want a gas-house-gang type of club this year. Do I make myself clear?"

"Yeah," Ed Lubec answered, and grinned. "We get tough especially against the Moguls, Ben. Am I right?"

"You said it, I didn't!" Macklin snapped, a small smile accompanying his words, then gave them the starting lineup that would be presented at the plate at one forty-five.

PATTON	SS
ERNENWINE	LF
LUBEC	CF
STECKMAN	1B
SPINNEY	RF

MCIVER	C
RAGONI	2B
BRAND	3B
VILA	P

Over forty thousand fans pressured the Gold Sox when they took the field for infield practice. Howie was amazed; his nervousness was back in the clubhouse, and the crowd was no different from others he had known. It was just that there were more of them here, giving out with their blaring voices and opinionated braying. He heard his own name shouted above the racket, and as he picked up a ground ball and fired it to Ragoni, a loud fan yelled, "The old Argonauts, yeah! You're still Are-nots, ha!"

Sitting in the dugout later, Howie watched the Bengals' heavy artillery put the shells into the stands. Knorr had the crowd roaring with his long bombs. He wished it were time. And soon it was and Macklin went out to meet Detroit's Dan Harmon to talk over the ground rules. Howie went to the bat rack and froze there while the National Anthem was played; when the organ music trailed off, the fans turned loose the old anticipatory blast of sound.

The volume grew and was run through with derisive boos when the little shortstop stepped in to the batter's box. The Bengal catcher lost no time in welcoming him to major league ball, as rough as the law allowed. "Hi, rabbit, what big ears you got!"

Waggling his thick-stemmed bat, his jaw thrust out, Howie looked out at Masi. The first pitch came in tight. He moved back, and the Detroit fans yelled with delight when the strike was called. Masi moved the ball around, inside and outside, and Howie stayed with him, running the count full. The Bengal infielders moved back a little. Then he shortened up and bunted Masi's payoff pitch between the mound and third base.

132

He flew up the line, crossed the bag ahead of Masi's desperate throw, and felt savage satisfaction in the sudden break in the crowd's razzing.

Howie, with Ernenwine at bat, kept Masi in a stew with his threatened breaks toward second. He took off when Ernenwine swung at a one and two pitch and rifled it to third. The throw to second to start the double play was just too late but, to make sure, the little shortstop barreled in at the Bengal second sacker and sent him sprawling. Randy Cote was an old veteran and his pride was hurt. He charged Howie as soon as he was on his feet. The Gold Sox shortstop ducked a wild swing, then got in and wrapped his arms around Cote's ribs. The umpires finally prevented a serious rhubarb and threatened to evict Cote and his manager, Dan Harmon.

The Detroit manager remembered that Lubec's pinch hitting last year with the Moguls included ten homers, and he waved his outfield back. Masi, after getting two strikes past the hitter, pulled the string. Lubec timed the pitch right and lofted it to short center, where the ball fell just out of reach of the onrushing Detroit fielder. The bases full and none out, the home crowd yelled for Harmon to take the pitcher out, then applauded Masi when he whipped a called third strike past Steckman. Wes Spinney, however, hit Masi's third pitch through the middle, scoring Howie and Stu Ernenwine. On the throw-in to the plate that nearly cut down the second run, Lubec raced to third, and the Detroit catcher's throw to that bag got past the third baseman and let Lubec come in. The crowd turned their wrath against the Bengals when Masi walked McIver, but a few moments later their mood changed quickly when Nick Ragoni hit into a double play.

Howie threw the Bengal leadoff man out, coming up with a hard shot to his right, Vila got ahead of the next batter with two quick called strikes, then brushed the Bengal third baseman with an inside pitch that brought a roar from the crowd.

133

Frank Knorr, Detroit's heavy hitter, stepped in, hitting from the left side of the plate. Howie yelled from short, "Get him, Felipe. He struck out over a hundred times last year!" For a moment he regretted the outburst, then Nick Ragoni was chattering, and Steckman shouted, "Burn it by him, amigo!"

Vila blazed a pitch in, on the outside corner and high enough. He jammed Knorr with an inside pitch that was called the second strike, and the Bengal belter stepped out and got dirt on his hands, the crowd imploring him to hit the next pitch out of sight. Vila threw a waste pitch, then missed the plate with a half speed curve. Knorr tied into the next pitch and the crowd came up roaring as Wes Spinney ran toward the barrier in right. He jumped high, spun half around, and made a backhand catch that slammed thousands of excited fans back onto their seats.

The cry for the long bomb burst forth again when Jacoby, the Bengals' cleanup hitter, dug in at the plate. Last year he had trailed Knorr by only seven circuit clouts. Felipe Vila stayed with the slugger, got the count out all the way, then struck him out on a pitch that was low and wide of the plate.

Alex Brand started off the Gold Sox offensive in the top of the second by beating out a hit to deep short. After Felipe Vila waved feebly at a third strike, Howie stepped in, the Detroit fans and the Bengal bench loudly abusive. There was a smattering of applause that seemed apologetic and was of short duration.

Masi, still shaken by the events of the previous inning, glowered at the Gold Sox leadoff man. He fired a pitch in well above the letters, missed with a slider, then reared back and threw his fast ball. "Look out!" he yelled, even as the ball left his fingers, but the ball hit Howie on the shoulder before he could hit the dirt. The shortstop got up, grinning, and trotted to first, and the Detroit first baseman, Jacoby, gave him a crooked smile and said, "So far you're lucky, busher!"

134

"Yeah, maybe," Howie bit out, keeping his eyes away from the man.

Masi looked out at the Detroit bullpen and chewed harder on his gum. One more hit or a walk, he knew, and he was out of there. He bowed his neck and struck out Ernenwine and then got Ed Lubec on a long fly to right center.

Felipe Vila got by until the last of the fifth, when he walked Lessinger, number two man in the Bengal lineup, then served up a gopher ball that Knorr lost in the right-field seats. There were two men on and one out when Howie Patton flagged down a hard grounder and turned it into a double play.

The Gold Sox had men on in the next two innings but could not bring them in, and then Jacoby tied the ball game up in the eighth with a tremendous blast into the left-field seats. When the Cleveland team came in for their cuts in the first of the ninth, Ernie Bolan came away from the drinking fountain, a sour smile on his lips. "That was a beaut of a bunt by Jacoby. The loudest I ever heard."

Macklin said, when Spinney left the bat rack, "Get a good ball, Wes. Hit it good but don't try to murder it, and then it might go all the way."

The ex-Mogul right fielder swung at Masi's first pitch and drove it inside the left-field line for a stand-up double, and the Detroit manager was out of the dugout in a hurry. An old fireman named Yerbe took the long walk in and Masi handed him the ball and left the mound, muttering under his breath. McIver waited Yerbe out and finally walked, and the crowd howled their impatience. When Yerbe wild-pitched both base runners along, he was through. The Bengals' third pitcher, Rundlett, after his warmups, brought the crowd into a good mood once more by striking out Alex Brand and Fairbrother, hitting for Vila. Howie stepped in to hit, the fans calling for his scalp. He grinned a little when one yelled, "Get that little pest!"

135

Howie ran his hands up the handle of his bat and swung at the first pitch, fouling it off. He let a ball go by, then bunted foul, and the Detroit first baseman moved back. Rundlett fired a change-up in and the stands rocked as Lubec streaked for the plate with the pitch. Howie bunted, sending a trickler out onto the grass between the mound and the third-base line. He was halfway to first, building up speed, when the pitcher scrambled for the ball. When he had it, he stood in his tracks, knowing he was too late to make a play.

It was the run that meant the ball game, and in the visitors' dressing room Howie tried desperately to be matter-of-fact about it all as his teammates showered him with congratulations. Three hits in four official trips to the plate for the man who used to dream of this hour as a kid back in Hagersville! Macklin let the writers in, and the veteran scribe traveling with the Gold Sox gave the manager an expansive grin. "A good start, Ben. They looked great out there today. You've got the wheels, all right. Where's Patton?"

The little shortstop hurried into the shower room, remembering what this same Garvin had written a couple of days ago. He doubted that the new Cleveland club would prove their point through the hot nights and the sun-baked afternoons when the pressure of the pennant race reached its height. Other go-go teams had had their hearts broken by a Series sweep by the Moguls and had never bounced back. The Gold Sox just did not figure to finish better than seventh.

When he came out to dress he heard Bolan's voice. "Trafton hit two today against the Gophers, Wes. Think you'll ever ride in a Cadillac or shave for a TV audience?"

Spinney tossed a beverage can aside and showed Bolan the ragged edge of his temper. "Don't you ever shut your big mouth?" he fired back. "I've seen some fresh rookies but——"

"Sor-ry!" Bolan said. "Just kidding, Wes." He took his sports coat out of his locker and headed for the door. Ed

Lubec and Steckman were waiting for him, and Lubec said something to the rookie and laughed. Here, Howie thought, were signs of boring from within, the surreptitious jab here, the sly dig there where a man was most vulnerable. He could tell Macklin a lot about Bolan that had never been in a scout's report, but he knew he'd have to let the Gold Sox pilot find out for himself. He hoped it would be soon—not too late.

11

THE GOLD SOX MADE IT TWO STRAIGHT OVER the Bengals, Macklin using Bert Kahl in a surprise move that paid off. The man peering through heavy lenses set the opposition down 5-1, with Howie Patton stealing two bases. They moved on to the nation's capital for a three-game set with the Washington Solons and swept it, and the sports writers began reaching into their bags of superlatives to descibe the play of Macklin's motley crew, especially the recklessness of men like Patton, Ernenwine, and Alex Brand on the bases. Even the big league castoffs, Spinney and Ragoni, seemed to have found new wheels.

The long ball buffs everywhere still had to be shown, and they were patiently and fiendishly waiting for the Go-go Gold Sox to arrive at the Mogul stadium on the 27th of April. A New York columnist said the new Cleveland club could only be described as "Crazy, man, crazy." Their base-running put him in mind of the Kamikaze suicide pilots of the last war. Macklin had shortened the swings of potential home-run hitters like Lubec, Spinney, and Steckman. How long would he make them like it? No sane manager on the other clubs could anticipate Macklin's next move, no matter what the situation called for in the baseball book. Patton, the rookie, was blazing, but he'd bet the canny veteran behind the plate for the Moguls would cool him off.

Nearly forty thousand fans turned out under the lights when the Gold Sox appeared for the first time in their own ball park, and Howie warmed to the deafening outburst of applause as he ran out to take the field against Detroit. He yelled in at Al "Razor" Burk, Macklin's starting pitcher; called over to Alex Brand at third. He ran over to second base and slapped Nick Ragoni on the back; scampered back to short when the Bengal leadoff man dug in at the plate. He was taking charge. That morning he had received a letter from home that said Sam McCloud had suffered another attack but was holding on well.

The bony man with the scythe was trying to throw his stuff past McCloud, but the veteran would hang on, Howie felt sure, until he learned the truth, one way or the other. . . . The Detroit hitter had gone back to the dugout to change bats and the fans were strafing him. Howie thought of a line he'd read in the morning paper. "Patton, the new Cleveland shortstop, seems to play with a deadly intensity, a determination that makes you believe he's fighting for a cause." It had turned his thinking around, and he knew now that he had not fought his way to the big leagues in two short years just to spite his father or Sam McCloud. . . .

Al Burk was ready to pitch, and the usual roar came from the crowd as he fired a strike past the hitter. The control pitcher hit the outside corner with a curve that was swung at and missed, and the batter stepped out and reached for some dirt.

The shortstop knew his increasing purpose was one with McCloud's and Frank Leggett's. A five-foot seven rookie, an old journeyman ballplayer and a multimillionaire had a cause: to take the emphasis off the home run; to bring the game of baseball back to what it should be, a game of varying skills forgotten by most of the present-day scouts and fans. . . .

139

Burk's next pitch was rammed back through his legs, and Howie raced to his left and scooped the ball up behind the keystone sack, threw off balance to Steckman, and beat the runner by a step. The racket that went up was for Frank Knorr moving into the on-deck circle, Howie knew, not the fielding gem. He moved to his left a little, and Alex Brand played close to the foul line. The Bengal number two hitter could pull the ball. With the count two and nothing, he hit a vicious shot too hot for Brand to handle cleanly, but he did deflect it toward short where Howie pounced on it and fired to Steckman, missing the base runner by half a step. The roar went up when Knorr stepped in.

Burk took his time between pitches. He called McIver out to get the signs straight, after the slugger had worked the count to three balls and one strike.

The Gold Sox shortstop could think of a hundred ballplayers, if he took the time, who had performed with great skill both in the field and at the plate through many seasons, but how many of them had received due recognition then or were remembered now? They'd simply moved in the shadows of the .270 hitting muscle men. Who cared about the ones who scored ahead of the sluggers? They were just the runs batted in. . . .

The fans came up when Knorr blasted a long foul into the left-field stands, and then, with the count full, Burk gave Knorr a big motion, pulled the string, and struck him out. Al Burk paid little attention to the runner at first for the Bengal cleanup hitter, Jacoby, was digging in at the plate. He fired a fast ball in and then winced at the sound of Jacoby's bat, turned, and watched the ball drop into the right center-field bleachers. Howie watched Jacoby all the way around the bases and into the Bengal dugout. They said he was paid nearly sixty thousand a year.

Burk got the next man out on a high foul to McIver, and the fans were still buzzing over Jacoby's blast when the Gold Sox

140

reached the dugout. Their mood changed when Howie moved in to start off the last half of the inning. The chant, "Go—go—go!" rose up as Howie let the first pitch go by. It began to taper off when he got behind Dario Masi, one ball and two strikes, then turned into a massed groan of disappointment when he flied to shallow right. The Bengal pitcher struck out Ernenwine and Lubec.

For five innings the Go-go Gold Sox had gone nowhere. Masi had limited them to two scratch hits, and in the top of the sixth Knorr, first up, rocketed Al Burk's first pitch into the bleachers. Even though Burk retired the next three men, the crowd got on the Gold Sox when they came in for their bats. "Bring back the old team!" a stout-lunged fan behind the home dugout yelled. "Go—go—go back to the bushes!"

Macklin nodded to Janosek, and the infielder went in to hit for Al Burk, the crowd jeering the manager's move. Masi got Janosek to hit his pitch to short but the Detroit fielder pulled the first baseman off the bag with a low throw and the runner was on. Digging in at the plate for his third time at bat, Howie tried not to let the boos and the verbal abuse from the stands rile him. Masi jammed him with a fast ball, whistled one in close to his chin that sat him down in the dirt. When he got set again, he saw the Bengal infield move in to guard against the bunt.

Masi threw a slow curve and Howie quickly shifted his feet and swung, riding the ball to the right-field corner a foot inside the line. He rounded first and picked up speed. He was past second as Janosek, waved in by Cy Turkin, drew the throw to the plate. The Bengal catcher had to take the throw four feet up the first-base line, and he had no chance to tag Janosek. He fired a bullet to third, but Howie was there well ahead of the ball. The Cleveland fans took full advantage of their first chance to howl. Now they were yelling in unison, "Go—go—Gold Sox!"

With Ernenwine at bat, Howie tantalized Masi with his long

leads off third. The Detroit ace missed the plate with his first three pitches. When Ernenwine swung and missed at a slider, the Detroit catcher rifled a throw to third that caromed off the fielder's glove. Howie raced in to the plate with Cleveland's second run, and the stands began to rock. Masi lost Ernenwine, and Ed Lubec, given the green light, swung hard at the second pitch and drove it between right and center for a triple. Macklin let Steckman swing but Masi struck him out, and the Bengal outfield moved back when Spinney, the ex-Mogul, dug his spikes into the dirt of the batter's box.

Spinney ran the string out, fouled off five straight pitches, then took a lazy cut at a change of pace and looped it out into shallow right, where the outfielder tried a shoestring catch. The ball skipped by him and Lubec scored the run that tied up the game, Spinney going to second. Masi purposely passed Cass McIver to set up a double play, and a few moments later Nick Ragoni dumped a bunt up the first-base line and beat it out, and the bases were full. The Cleveland fans were delirious when Macklin sent Lew Mintzer out to hit in the pitcher's spot. The Detroit manager came out to the mound and signaled for a fireman.

On the bench, Howie threw a glance at Ernie Bolan, who had growled impatiently when the nod had gone to Mintzer. He could almost hear the rookie's blood boil above the steady roar of sound filling the big ball park. Then he looked out at the action again. The relief pitcher was ready to work on Mintzer. He was a "junkman," the bane of sluggers. Mintzer swung twice and missed, then chopped at a pitch and hit it between the plate and the mound, the ball bouncing a good twenty feet in the air, Spinney scoring while the third baseman waited for the ball to come down.

Up for the second time, Howie heard the chant, "Go, go, Gold Sox!" Somewhere in the stands a crazy combo was giving out with doubtful music. He looked up the line for Turkin's sign, then choked up on the bat and dug in. He liked the first pitch and cut at it, sent a little blooper over the pitcher's head that the Bengal shortstop had to cut over for. He made a terrific play, but his snap throw failed to get the speedy Gold Sox shortstop, and another run scored. Gold Sox 5, Detroit 3.

Stu Ernenwine grounded sharply to the Bengal second baseman, forcing Howie at second by a hair, but the little base runner ruined the shortstop's attempt to complete the double play with a slide that took Cote's feet from under him. The sixth Gold Sox run scored, and the partisan crowd went nearly mad.

Ed Lubec, allowed to swing away, flied deep to left, ending the visitors' agony.

With Mitch Moger working the rest of the way, the Gold Sox won it, 8-5, Frank Knorr hitting his second home run in the top of the ninth.

Late the next morning, Ernenwine went out and picked up the newspapers. When he got back, he gave Howie a big smile. "Know what he's calling you now, that Garvin? 'Patton, the Little General, is the spark that touches off the fire under the other players, the take-charge guy.' "

Howie reached for the paper, turned it quickly to the sports page. A headline said, "GOLD SOX WIN. Knorr Blasts Two!" He laughed. "Well, they mention us in the fine print, Stu."

The second game was rained out, and the Gold Sox flew to Kansas City, where they won two out of three and took over the league lead from the Moguls. On the way to Baltimore they caught up with current statistics. Trafton had six homers and was conceded a good chance of beating the record, along with Torkl, Knorr and half a dozen others. Howie, with five stolen bases already chalked up, wondered if the writers and their public would ever remember the record set in that department. The plane whooshed down, then rose up as head winds hit it. Alex Brand said, "I hope that's no sign we're going into a slump."

"We'll find out in New York," Ernie Bolan called from the seat he shared with Lubec back toward the tail, and there was a quality in the laughter of certain players that was not conductive to high morale. In the hotel in Kansas City, a rumor had circulated for a while saying that Ollie Spicer, Bolan, and one or two other players had gone to Macklin's suite demanding to be played or traded.

"The Moguls?" Steckman remarked. "Didn't you guys ever hear of a guy licking a grizzly bear with a buggy whip?"

"It'll be O.K." Bolan laughed. "Haven't we got the Little General? Little old blood and guts?" Howie got up from his seat, fire in his eyes, but Ernenwine yanked him back. Macklin's voice roared the length of the DC-8. "Knock it off, Bolan! A few more cracks like that and you'll be back in Grand Rapids!"

"Maybe you'd like to make a bet on that," the rookie said, then lapsed into silence.

Ernenwine leaned close to Howie. "Looks like there was more to that rumor than we thought." The shortstop nodded, remembering his first two clashes with Bolan, simply physical ones. The next one that seemed sure to come, he thought, would not be resolved as easily. It was one take-charge guy against the other, each with radically different motives.

A virus bug hit Stu Ernenwine three hours before the night game with the Bluejays, and he was ordered to stay in bed. Macklin put Ernie Bolan in left. A big crowd came out to see this unorthodox team with all the wheels but experienced no undue excitement until the top of the fifth, when Nick Ragoni singled off the Baltimore southpaw. Larry Dru, attempting to lay one down, popped out to the backstop, and Howie Patton, showered by mixed cheers and boos, singled to right on a three and nothing pitch, sending Ragoni to third.

144

Ernie Bolan, making his every move a picture, strode to the plate. He threw two of his three bats away and squared off against Rosson. Howie, taking his lead off first, the fans yelling at him to dare and try to steal, knew Bolan's orders were just to meet the ball. The blond rookie fouled a pitch off, then swung from his heels, the ball soaring high above the infield where the Bluejay shortstop gathered it in.

Ed Lubec, in a slump, was long overdue. He guarded the plate until he got the ball he wanted, a curve that hung just long enough for him to drill it to left center. Howie, running, caught a glimpse of the Bluejay fielder bobbling the ball in the corner for a moment. He wheeled around third and slid across the plate just as the throw-in smacked into the catcher's mitt. Lubec raced to third. He died there when Steckman looked at a third strike.

Larry Dru kept his whitewash brush going. In the eighth, Howie beat out a bunt, raced to second when the pitcher overthrew first base, then scampered home on a single by Lubec in short center despite a beeline throw to the plate. The Baltimore fans gave him a round of applause as he jogged to the dugout. He caught Bolan's sullen glance before he went to the drinking fountain. The Gold Sox left the field with a 3-0 triumph, while over thirty thousand people poured toward the exits, most of them shaking their heads over what they had seen.

The Gold Sox lost the second game in the seventh inning, when it seemed they might draw even. With none out, Felipe Vila, the pitcher, nicked the Bluejay pitcher for one of his infrequent hits, and Howie blooped a hit over second. Ernie Bolan stepped to the plate, the bunt sign on, and the Baltimore infield acted accordingly. Bolan missed the first pitch as he shortened up, and then he watched a curve hit an inside corner for the second strike.

Keeping his stuff high, the Bluejay right-hander burned a

pitch in around the letters, and Bolan took a full cut and drove it deep to right, where the Bluejay right fielder picked it out of the stands with a leaping stab. Vila and Howie tagged up and took the extra base, but Lubec, also swinging from his heels, popped up to the infield. It was the Gold Sox's last big chance and they lost, 4-1. Macklin jawed at Bolan all the way to the visitors' dressing room. He promised him a stiff fine the next time he ran things his own way.

"Nuts!" Bolan said, when he ripped off his shirt. "I was an inch away from knotting that game up. That makes me a bum? You've been lucky so far, Macklin. You and your bunts on third strike! You'll have us swinging in New York, mister, believe me!"

"I wouldn't," the manager said, "not under oath," and walked away, leaving Bolan steaming in his anger and his sweat.

The Gold Sox took the rubber game 6-2, winning on just five hits, but they ran wild on Bluejay errors, made use of every base on balls, and capitalized on two stolen bases. The lobby of the hotel in New York was swarming with writers when the Gold Sox checked in on April 27th. "They're ready for you, Ben," a *Post-Telegram* scribe said. "Hasler has his pitching staff primed."

"He'll see some chuckers, too," the manager said dryly. "Tell him to keep his bullpen hot."

They singled Howie out. How did the Little General feel? Would the pressure of the Mogul stadium and all it stood for affect him?

"It's just another ball park," Howie snapped back.

The writers embellished and exaggerated the little short-stop's remark to the limit of their elastic consciences. The Argonaut rookie, the Little General of the Gold Sox, was a confirmed Mogul hater as far back as he could remember. He'd play his heart out against what they stood for.

146

Howie got a postcard in the mail the next morning. It was from Sam McCloud and the shaky handwriting sobered him for a few minutes. It said, "Run 'em ragged, kid. I'm hangin' on just to get that laugh."

The pressure was there in the Mogul three-tiered stadium when Howie moved out of the dugout to lead off for the Gold Sox. Out of the seats came the loudest massed human cry he had ever heard. For the most part it was a scornful welcome, and before he got into earshot of the heckling Mogul catcher, the smattering of polite applause was completely muffled by the booing, the catcalls, of over forty thousand fans. Digger Lowney, the Mogul catcher, said scornfully, "So you're the pop-off shrimp!"

"How is the chow in the old men's home?" Howie fired back at the face behind the mask, and Lowney spat into the dirt and hunkered down. The roar of the crowd stepped up when Hasler's ace left-hander, Rusty Kroll, threw a strike past the hitter. The Mogul bench jockeys hammered their jibes at Howie through the sound. Kroll caught the outside corner of the plate with a curve, and Lowney said, "You won't see a piece of his stuff all afternoon, big mouth."

He waited Kroll out, fouled off a three and two payoff pitch, then clubbed a fast ball that caromed off the left-hander's shin and rolled toward the third-base line. Before the ball was picked up, Howie was on first, and he stood there and watched the Mogul trainer come out and check Kroll. The pitcher limped around, glaring over at the base runner. He threw a few practice pitches before he nodded to Lowney. The Mogul first baseman, Jumbo Hauser, holding Howie on, said under his breath. "Look out I don't stomp you down, Junior."

Stu Ernenwine, healthy again, guessed right on Kroll's first three pitches. The Mogul manager came out to the mound,

147

meeting Lowney there, and the shortstop joined the huddle. Apparently, Howie thought, that ball I hit has got him out. He heard Hauser's threat of reprisal behind him when Kroll limped toward the Mogul bench, and caught a note of anxiety in the muted roar of the crowd.

The relief pitcher got a strike past Ernenwine and then walked him. Lubec hit a short fly to right, and the Mogul fielder lazily threw the ball in. Howie tagged up, then streaked for third, paralyzing the Mogul second baseman for a moment. He threw to third and seemed to have the runner cut down, but Howie came in hard and dumped the infielder, making him lose the ball. Ernenwine went into second.

Steckman struck out, and then Wes Spinney, nothing on his mind save evening things with the team that had turned him loose, slashed a double down the left-field line to drive in two runs.

After Cass McIver lined out, the Mogul fans witnessed a brand of baseball that had them on their feet most of the time. In the fifth, the Moguls unleashed their power and went ahead, on a double and back-to-back homers by the T-men, Trafton and Torkl. The Go-go Gold Sox evened it up in the sixth without a hit. Howie Patton walked, stole second, moved to third on Ernenwine's fly to right, and scored on another long out made by Lubec. The Mogul catcher, Lowney, ripped a line-drive homer into the right-field seats, just three hundred feet away, in the eighth, and then the Gold Sox started wheeling again.

Nick Ragoni singled off the fourth Mogul pitcher, to start the visitors off in the ninth, and Howie, with the crowd still calling for his scalp, drew the Mogul infield in with two bunt attempts, then punched a single over short. Lubec dug in, glared over at the Mogul dugout he knew so well, then smashed a long drive to left that cleared the bases. George Hasler called time and brought in another pitcher, an old

148

veteran. Steckman, Spinney, and Cass McIver went down before him, and the fans yelled for Mogul power to pull the game out.

Ben Macklin called Sal Sava in to pitch the ninth. After getting the first Mogul hitter, he turned wild and walked the next two men. Trafton stepped in and Macklin ordered him put on, gambling on the double play. Sava pitched low, and Torkl rifled the next pitch between third and short that looked like the ball game until Howie Patton dived for it and caught it backhanded. He fired to Alex Brand from a sitting position and completed the twin killing.

Howie Patton felt thousands of pairs of eyes boring into him as he raced off the diamond, very happy that looks could not kill. When he ducked down out of sight he heard the applause break out and was certain it was not for him.

The New York fans watched the Gold Sox run like crazy again the next night and beat Hasler's starter, Johnny Steen, 6-0. They kept waiting in vain for the Mogul power to explode against Larry Dru's sidearm pitching, but the ex-Argonaut hurler completely silenced the T-men while his own mates pounded out two doubles and a triple to account for their run total. Rain fell all the next day and the Gold Sox moved into Chicago to play the Blue Sox. George Hasler made a statement to the press just after Macklin's club left town. "The Gold Sox script is a repeat. Two years ago, the Blue Sox had their honeymoon during the early weeks; last year, the Bluejays. We'll give them our dust in midsummer."

July fourth was the day of superstition in the big leagues. The team on top at that time would most likely be the pennant winner by October first. The Gold Sox moved into Baltimore for two games on July third, still ahead of the Moguls three games and a half, and the talk of both leagues. For the first time since opening day, the experts took time

149

out from raving about the home-run derby between Trafton, Torkl, Gruber and Knorr to make the public aware of Howie Patton's amazing total of stolen bases. The season half gone, the Gold Sox speed demon had thirty-eight to his credit, a blistering pace that revived memories of earlier days. Ernenwine, Brand, Ragoni, and Spinney had sixty-eight thefts between them. "Patton's beginning to take the glamor off the big blast," Garvin, the Cleveland writer, wrote for syndication. "The fans are coming out to watch him go, to hear his shrill voice as he fires up the other players. Off the field he's a mild-mannered and nicely spoken kid, but in his business suit he's made no friends and has truly earned the title of Little Blood and Guts."

Lacing his spikes in the dressing room at the Baltimore stadium, Howie tried to shake off the unease that had been creeping up on him for the past few days. A certain bogeyman trails every ball club, known to the trade as the Slump. More often than not, especially if it happens to a Cinderella team like the Gold Sox, it proves disastrous. Morale slumps accordingly, and the front office begins to probe, questioning the manager's ability, believing all the gripes from the players, and agreeing with the criticisms projected by the working press.

The strain of the race was in the faces of all the players around Howie, and he knew the question that kept pounding inside their heads. How much longer could they continue playing over their heads with the power-laden Moguls and Bengals thundering so close behind? Tempers were getting shorter, and day by day the sullenness among the reserves on the bench became more pronounced. Ernie Bolan was much too tractable to suit Howie; the man put him in mind of a buzzard perched on a high limb waiting for a stricken thing to die.

He had to keep them alive. He began with Bert Kahl, who

150

was polishing the thick lenses of his glasses, telling him he was a cinch to be an umpire when he quit pitching. The reaction was not too encouraging. He thought of Sam McCloud. "O.K., if I'd known I was attending a wake tonight, I'd have baked a cake! You've won half a pennant, you guys, and that's better than we expected. If the Moguls win out we'll sue for half the Series take. Come on, get the lead out and show the Bluejays what good losers we are!"

McIver stuffed scrap into his cheek and grinned. "Let's knock their tail feathers out," he said.

The Baltimore fans gave up in the seventh with the score 5-0 in favor of the Go-go Gold Sox, and Howie Patton on second with only one out. Many of them were moving toward the runways when the Little General raced to third on a short fly ball to right by Ernenwine. Howie had walked and stole second, his second theft of the night.

The crowd's noise rose when Lubec grounded out, then fell again when Steckman singled through the box and drove Howie in. A few minutes later the Bluejays came in, hardly a chirp coming from their bench, still hoping to break through Al Burk's stuff. From his shortstop post, Howie talked it up to the Gold Sox, ribbed the Bluejay hitter stepping in, yelled his defiance to the jockeys in the home dugout. Burk fired a ball and a strike in, and then the ball came scorching at Howie and he dug it out and threw the first man out. He kept chattering, a magpie harassing the Bluejays.

Al Burk lost the number two hitter in the Bluejay lineup, and then the power moved in. Baltimore's Jim McQueen, with nineteen homers at the plate; Polinski, the cleanup hitter, in the on-deck circle. McQueen, a left-handed pull hitter, cut into Burk's second offering and slammed it right at Nick Ragoni. Howie took the second baseman's throw, then went flying when the Bluejay base runner hit him with a rolling block. The crowd's noise quickly ebbed as the shortstop

151

went sprawling, but it turned into an admiring round of applause when Howie got to his feet in a hurry and ran back to his position.

Al Burk looked out at Howie and shouted, "I'll get this guy for that, kid." He threw a slow curve in that caught a corner, missed with a low fast ball, then sat Polinski down with another blazer close to his chin. The crowd was still booing when he cut the big slugger down, swinging. Hundreds more got up and moved to the exits, and the papers the next morning showed them they hadn't missed a thing, unless it was Howie Patton's second hit of the game in the ninth.

Howie had Tom Donohue look at the small spike wound just below the knee when he reached the dressing room. "One more day gone by," he yelled at the others, "and we're still alive!"

"I'm not layin' bets on how long *you'll* live," Wes Spinney shot back. "I'll bet there's a bounty on you."

Howie laughed. "Ever hear of anybody makin' lemonade without slicing some lemons? About that homer you hit in the fourth, Wes. You took a half swing, so tell me again they haven't hypoed the ball!"

"Nuts, Howie, I've got the power. Isn't that what that Mogul announcer says of everybody when he comes to the plate?"

The ensuing laugher lessened the sting of the medication the trainer applied to Howie's raw wound, but the little shortstop still had his fingers crossed when he got into his street clothes. He smelled a roadblock not far ahead. Just before the team had left Cleveland for this trip, Ernie Bolan had bought himself a sedan of a make often referred to as a status symbol. It was cream-colored and had his initials on the door. How many guys had rich uncles? How soon can a guy have it made?

He watched a certain group leave the dressing-room to-

152

gether—Bolan, Lubec, Spicer, Steckman, and Janosek—a faction that had been inseparable for weeks and hardly in love with Ben Macklin, and he told himself he'd give back ten of his stolen bases to get inside their minds.

It began on July 28th in Oakland, with the Gold Sox just two and a half games ahead of the Moguls. At the end of the fifth inning of the first night game, Howie read the ominous signs. Nick Ragoni, usually a brick wall at second, had committed two errors that gave the Oaks three unearned runs. The place hitters were not finding the holes to drive the ball through, and every break was in favor of the other team. Let down by a ragged defense, Larry Dru's control went sour and he left the mound in the fifth with two men on and nobody out. The first hitter to face reliever Danny Wade smashed a home run to the right field seats and the score was Oaks 8, Gold Sox 0.

Howie had a bad night himself. Twice the Oaks' catcher had cut him down, and he could not buy a hit. The fans ripped the Gold Sox up one side and down the other, reminding them that they were getting slaughtered by the team their city had considered expendable.

They went off the field smarting under the worst defeat of the season, 12-1, Ernie Bolan's home run preventing a shutout in the ninth. The rookie was the only man smiling when the team peeled off.

"It's one ball game," Macklin shouted at them. "You'd think we never lost one before! There's tomorrow; we'll get it back!"

When he came out of the shower room, Howie heard Ragoni arguing with Bolan. "Sure, you've been a lucky stiff, and maybe I am a pushover like you say, but the worm turns, Ernie. I'll get it back double when——"

"Knock it off!" Steckman warned when the door of the

visiting manager's office swung open. Howie's brows were knitted as he reached into his locker for his street shoes.

Oakland made it two straight the next night, their power hitters working Burk, Moger, and Sal Sava over for eight runs. Howie's two singles and another stolen base were given little recognition by the writers, who concentrated on predicting the beginning of the end for the Go-go Gold Sox. They were totally ignorant of what had taken place three hours after the Cleveland club had left the stadium.

Alex Brand and Cass McIver burst into the room Howie shared with Ernenwine an hour before noon. Howie said, "What in the world has happened, Alex? Leggett sell out already?"

"We're on the same floor as Bolan and Steckman," McIver said, his breathing labored. "About three o'clock this morning we heard some kind of ruckus, and we opened the door and sneaked a listen. It was Macklin raiding a poker game, and brother, some heads could drop!"

Howie's lips stretched tight and he nodded. "I suspected something like this. A deck of cards takes a lot of sleep away and stirs up hard feelings."

"Planned that way?" Alex Brand remarked.

"I don't want to believe that," McIver said. "I know one thing. Macklin will tear loose before tonight's game."

The Gold Sox got the message from Macklin to be at the ballpark a half hour earlier than usual, and when they were all there, the manager locked the doors against the writers.

"All right," Macklin said, his voice razor-edged, "I'm cracking the whip. There'll be bed checks at twelve o'clock, no card playing anywhere, and if you think I don't mean business, try me! It'll cost you a hundred bucks to find out. No wonder some of you are beginning to play like humpty-dumpties. Lubec, your eyes look like two poached eggs swimming in catsup. Steckman, a few more cans of brew and you'll have to

154

buy a girdle, so I'm giving you just ten days to get some of the suet off." He leveled his smoldering eyes at Ernie Bolan. "I'm sure you're the troublemaker, rookie, so get it out of your thick skull that you'll always be a white-haired boy!"

"I don't know what you mean, sir," Bolan said, so innocently that it was almost insulting.

"Riker, you'll take over first base tonight," Macklin said, "Mintzer, you'll be in center. Cortena is playing second. It'll give the poker players a chance to get the card pips out of their eyes."

Lubec said, "How long do you think you can bench me, Macklin?"

"As long as the Mogul manager did, Ed."

That night the Gold Sox came back to life, Lew Mintzer hitting a long double that meant the ball game, after Howie and Ernenwine got on with back-to-back singles. Something happened in the first of the eighth when the Gold Sox came in for their times at bat. Lubec, on his way to the drinking fountain, stepped on Howie Patton's foot and nicked him with his spikes. The shortstop wanted to believe, like all the other players did, that it was an accident. "Watch it, you jughead!" the manager snapped at the center fielder.

"Sure, I did it on purpose," Lubec growled. "Maybe I'll have better luck next time."

12

THE GOLD SOX FLEW BACK TO CLEVELAND, ONLY half a game ahead of the steadily driving Moguls, to open a two-game series with the Chicago Blues and the long-dreaded slump began. They dropped seven straight and fell into third place, and all over the circuit the experts came out with the same "we told you so" pitch. George Hasler, his Moguls in the lead by four games, magnanimously gave the fading Gold Sox credit for hanging on until August. Garvin, the veteran Cleveland columnist, said the Little General had carried the troops on his back as far as he could, and no matter what happened, he had to be considered one of the finest rookies of the year.

"With over six weeks left," he wrote, "Howie Patton has already stolen 53 bases, an incredible performance. He is hitting .289, has driven in 47 runs in the leadoff spot, and scored 59 himself. He refuses to crack under the pressure that seems to have caught up with most of the others on the Gold Sox club. . . . Rumors that there is dissension on the Cleveland club are too insistent to be ignored. . . ."

When the Gold Sox left their home park to begin a road trip in Minnesota, they were counted out of the pennant race, and Howie, staring out of the plane window, grinned dismally at a big blob of gossamer that broke away from the cloud mass and told himself it was the cloud nine he had been riding since April. The night before, he had received a card from Sam McCloud that said, "I'm still hanging on, kid. Don't forget the little cucumber does a lot of its fighting when it's on the ground. Remember it is most likely in the pickle barrel *next year*."

Next year. It never came for a lot of people.

Ernenwine brought him out of his bleak musings, although the left fielder's voice was kept low. "I'm sure of it now, Howie. Certain players are dogging it. They're swinging at any kind of a pitch, loafing in the field."

"I think you're right, Stu."

"Macklin ought to know it, unless he's dumber than I thought. But maybe he's given up on Leggett's type of baseball, Howie."

The Gold Sox took only one game of three with the Gophers, and broke even with Detroit. They moved into Chicago on August 25th, still in third place, seven and a half games behind the Moguls, and that night, Howie lifted his stolen bases total to sixty-one, keeping the big crowd yelling as much for him as it did for Knorr and Jacoby, the home-run hitters. In the field the Little General kept up a steady chatter, desperately trying to revive the Gold Sox's jaded spirits. He was half the noise that boiled out of the Cleveland dugout.

The Blues were leading at the end of seven, 5-3, and then Howie led off with a bloop single over short. The hostile crowd yelled for him to go, hoping to see him cut down. He took off when the Chicago hurler turned loose his third pitch to Ernenwine and slid in ahead of the catcher's perfect throw. "Sixty-two!" a fan yelled and, dusting himself off on second, Howie smiled to himself. They were beginning to count something at last besides the long bombs.

Stu Ernenwine singled to deep left and Howie raced home,

and then Ed Lubec struck out, running his hitless string to nothing for seventeen. Macklin called Steckman back and nodded to Lew Mintzer. "Take a good cut," he said. "Get the pitch you like." Steckman came back and sat down, his eyes stormy.

Mintzer doubled and tied up the ball game, and then Lew Spinney, also long overdue, lofted the ball into the left-field seats and put the Gold Sox out in front, 7-5. When they came into the dressing room they learned that the Moguls had won two from the Boston Beaneaters. "We'll be on a treadmill the rest of the way," Ollie Spicer growled. "We could win ten straight and those guys would win thirteen."

At breakfast the next morning, Howie called Alex Brand's attention to Bolan's left hand. The reserve outfielder sat six tables away, but the patch of adhesive tape near the knuckles of his left hand could be noticed all the way across the dining room. "He didn't get in the game last night, Alex," the shortstop said.

"Maybe he tangled with somebody last night after the game," Brand said, and forgot about it. He peered out of the window. "Typical Chicago weather, Howie. I doubt if we play tonight."

Cy Turkin came by the table. "I'll buy that, Alex," he said. "Ben took the plane to Akron a while ago. Leggett sent for him and put me in charge until he gets back."

"Oh, oh," Howie said, and had no more appetite. "You don't think he'd fire Macklin this quick, Cy?"

"Consider the mortality rate of managers," the coach said, and moved on.

It rained hard all day and showed no signs of a letup at six o'clock. After the word came that there would be no night game, Howie settled down with the Chicago evening papers. Filled to the brim with the spoutings of the sports writers, he read a gossip column headlined After Dark, written

158

by one Betty Lansdale. One line of the drivel brought him straight up in his chair. He read it a second time, something pawing at the edge of his thinking.

"What big league ballplayer tangled with the camera cutie at The Green Hat, a North Side bistro, late last night? And since when have baseball stars shied at having their pictures taken?"

Howie kept mulling this morsel of gossip over and over inside his head, remembering that coincidence was as unreliable as a sore-armed southpaw. But the feeling inside him was persistent. It was a hunch that had to be followed through.

Alex Brand came in with Vic Riker, and the third baseman said, "There's a pretty good fight on tonight, Howie. We can pick up some ringside seats down at the newsstand in the lobby."

"No, thanks. I just happened to think of somebody I want to look up before we leave Chicago, Alex."

"She have a friend?" Riker asked, eyes lighting up.

Howie laughed. "That I wouldn't know, Vic."

It was close to eleven thirty when Howie got out of a cab, crossed the sidewalk, and took two steps down to the entrance of the Green Hat. He heard music pulsing somewhere in the dim background and had a moment of panic. He was a yokel here and had never before invaded this kind of world. A big doorman, wearing a Kelly green top hat, said, "Evening, friend. You're a little early. The place doesn't start jumping until after midnight."

The neon sign, the bulbs outlining the shape of a plug hat, blinked on and off above him. "Well, that's all right," he said, in a dry voice, "I just stopped in for a little while."

Past the checkroom, he was met by an oily-faced man in a tuxedo, who surveyed him a little dubiously. "Alone?"

Howie nodded, and was led to a table far from the combo

159

that was playing and the small waxed floor where a few couples were dancing. He wanted to run and was about to obey the impulse when a waiter placed a menu in front of him. He had to order something, he knew, and discovered the cheapest sandwich ran to three dollars. He ordered that and some ginger ale, and the waiter lifted his eyebrows at him as if he had done something terribly wrong.

He kept watching for the girl with the camera, and just after the waiter brought his order, he saw her. She was a dark-haired girl with eyes intriguingly aslant, and she wore a strapless evening gown covered with little doodads that glittered when she moved. She stopped by a table where a party of four were making their presence felt, and soon a flashlight bulb exploded. Howie knew he had to talk to her but wondered if any sound would come out of his throat if she gave him the chance. He paid strict attention to his sandwich, just about deciding to finish it fast and get out of there, when he caught the scent of perfume and heard the soft voice say, "Good evening, sir. Would you like to have your picture taken?"

He looked up at her, weakness like a sudden attack of virus coming over him. "Why—why, all right," he said. "You know, I—I came here just to talk to you."

She gave him a wary puzzled look.

He laughed uneasily and said hurriedly, "No, miss, it isn't that way. I came here because of a friend who was here last night. You had a little—well, trouble with him."

"Oh, him! I didn't know he was a ballplayer until I read that column in the paper. You know, you look very familiar."

"I'd like to talk to you if there's a place. . . ." Howie's voice was sticky in his throat.

"It's all right here. My time's my own," the girl said. "I have what you call a concession."

"The picture you took of him," Howie said, mustering up

160

courage. "He'd like to have it. After what happened he didn't feel like coming here himself so——"

"You stuck *your* neck out. The funny thing about it," the girl said, "is that he thinks I never did take his picture. I think he had a little too much to drink, and when he came out of the private room he saw me with the camera and jumped to conclusions. He made a try to tear it away from me and—well, I think I scratched him a little."

"You didn't take any picture?"

"Not that time. I took it after he'd gone into the private room with four other people. Sometimes I take a chance and get a candid picture, and ninety-nine times out of a hundred the customers are very pleased and pay what I ask. After what happened, though, I marked this one off as a dead loss."

"Like you said," Howie replied, "he was not quite himself, miss. I know he'd like to have it."

The girl beamed, her smile putting butterflies in Howie's chest. "This is my lucky night, mister. I'll be back in a few moments." She hesitated. "I get twenty dollars for a picture."

"It's a deal," the little shortstop said, hoping she would hurry up. Some of the customers were beginning to stare at him, and only that morning the papers had carried his picture on the sports pages. She was back in less than three minutes, sliding a glossy print out of a manila envelope, and Howie's heart pounded when he gave it a hurried glance. "That's it," he said, and reached for his billfold. "Thanks loads, miss. I hope I'll see you again."

"I'm generally here," the girl said. "Stop by when you're back in town."

"Oh, by the way," Howie said, as he paid the waiter. "Who owns this place?"

"Willie Grusso and Harry Kostuk." The waiter favored him with a wry smile. "Want to buy 'em out?"

On his way back to the hotel the cold grin he'd taken with

161

him from the Green Hat never left his face. Now, he knew, he would really take charge of the Gold Sox, and everything considered he still could boot them in. Cy Turkin rose out of a chair in the hotel lobby when he made his way to the elevators. "You!" the acting manager said, his cigar nearly slipping from his teeth. "Know what time it is?"

The shortstop glanced at his watch. It was twelve forty-five. "O.K., Cy," he said, "I know you have to report me."

Turkin sniffed at Howie's breath, then shook his head. "What could you possibly find to do this late when you've got no vices at all? Don't tell me, tell Ben."

"Sure, Cy, I'll give him the surprise of his not so young life."

"Ballplayers!" Turkin snorted. "They're not people." He trailed Howie all the way up to his room. "Say, you got a girl?"

"Seeing one doesn't mean you have one," Howie said. "Good night, Cy."

He put the photo in the bottom of his suitcase, got out of his clothes and into bed without waking Ernenwine, and lay awake for another hour. More than a few of the Gold Sox were aware of his edginess throughout most of the next day and feared that defeatism had begun to catch up with him. He called Macklin's suite four times before the man's voice answered. "I've got to see you," he said. "It's important."

"It had better be, kid," Macklin said. "I haven't had a nice trip. All right, get down here as quick as you can."

Macklin was in his dressing gown, chewing savagely on a cigar. "Sit down and spill it, Howie. If it's about you stayin' out, forget it. You would have to have a good reason."

"I sure did! But it may make you sick." He filled Macklin in on the piece of gossip he'd read, mentioned the tape on the back of Bolan's hand, then told him of his visit to the night club, before he took the photograph from the envelope.

Ben Macklin studied it closely when the shortstop placed

162

it in his hand. Shock built up quickly in his weathered face as he turned his eyes away from it for a moment to stare at Howie. The evidence of betrayal shook in his hand and anger began to grow in his eyes. He turned them to the photo again and spoke names. "Arnie Cashman, Engel, Bolan, Spicer, and Steckman!" He dropped into a chair, biting down hard on his cigar. "I suspected something, Howie, but certainly not this much." He laughed bitterly. "The Last Supper, but how many pieces of silver?"

Howie said, "It's Cashman's way of buying Leggett out, it seems to me. He could take his time ruining the club, then get it for his own price. Next year, maybe."

Macklin slammed a big fist against the arm of his chair. "The dirty, slimy conniver!" he ground out, then swung a fierce mirthless smile toward the shortstop. "This will finish him for good, I'll guarantee you that. You're right, kid, I'm sick to my stomach!" He got to his feet and paced the floor, suddenly stopped and asked, "You tell anybody about this?"

Howie shook his head.

"Ah, that's good," the manager said, and gave his star player a genuine smile. "You've held us up all year, and now I think you've saved us!" His mood abruptly changed when he stared at the photograph again. "The Green Hat, you said, kid. Oh, Arnie Cashman is a real smart operator. He figured he'd take no chances if he called a meeting at somebody else's club. Hah, and it was Ernie Bolan that boomeranged on him. You run along, Howie, and remember you know from nothing. We can't air this dirty linen where the public will see it. Leave the rest to me!" He shook his head. "General manager Ned Engel in with those rats. Can a guy trust his mother?"

"There had to be a reason for his not going to Oakland with the old Cleveland club," Howie said.

"We stop over in Washington before we go back home,

Howie, so things can't wait until then. We've got to clean house and start winning. I'll give out the word that the players are to report a half hour earlier at the ballpark. Meanwhile I'll make a couple of long distance calls. That's all, kid."

The Gold Sox were in the visitors' dressing room shortly after six thirty, wondering what announcement Macklin would make regarding his hurried trip to see the big boss. "Another pep talk," Ernie Bolan said. "The old razzmatazz. The do or die for old Chemro Tech."

Steckman laughed. "Wouldn't it be somethin' if Leggett told Macklin to try louder bats?"

Ernenwine, sitting next to Howie, said under his breath, "I think you know something."

"Maybe. Keep your shirt on, Stu."

The door to Macklin's cubicle swung open and the manager stepped out, a cold cigar jutting out from one corner of his mouth. "The doors," he said to the trainer. "They're posted out there? Cy and——?"

Donohue nodded.

"Bolan," the manager said, "where were you night before last—late?"

Howie, watching the rookie closely, saw a muscle in his face jump. Bolan steadied, forced a grin, and said, "On the town. So I lost a hundred."

"Who was with you at the Green Hat, Bolan?"

The outfielder's eyes showed the first sign of alarm. "Nobody, Macklin."

"You're a liar!" The manager removed the photograph from the envelope and held it up for all to see. "Come closer, Bolan, and get a look at it. You're nice and photogenic, but I can't say as much for Arnie Cashman, our general manager, Engel, or Spicer and Steckman."

"W-Where did you get that?" Bolan choked out, seeming

164

to shrink inside his silk summer suit. "Look, there was nothing to it. We were just——"

"Selling out the Gold Sox, you crumby dogs! How many more of your pals were on Cashman's payroll?"

The dressing room became deathly quiet for several dragged-out seconds. Suddenly Nick Ragoni got to his feet and made for Bolan. "You louse, I never thought——"

Howie grabbed the second baseman and held him off, but Wes Spinney yelled, "Let him go, kid. Let him beat his head in!"

"Knock it off!" Macklin snapped. "I've called Mr. Leggett and the commissioner. Cashman will be invited to the D.A.'s office sometime tomorrow, and it's my guess it will never go well for him to ever be recognized in a ball park for the rest of his life. A copy of this picture will be at the D.A.'s office the first thing in the morning. Others will be mailed out to the commissioner and the league president, and there will be a meeting of all concerned in Cleveland behind closed doors!"

Howie glanced at the players involved and almost felt sorry for Steckman. Bolan choked out, beads of sweat around his mouth, "Yeah? If we're dead ducks, Cashman will be, too. I'll sound off from here to——"

"You do that, Ernie," Macklin said. "I recall a couple of guys once, close to Arnie, who disappeared in a very mysterious manner. A bunch of rats dirtied up this game many years ago, and it took time for it to recover. This is the way it's going to be, Bolan: you and the other guilty ones will suit up for every game and keep your mouths shut, until we can dispose of you in our own way. Oh, you'll never play in the big leagues again. It'll be far out in the sticks or along the Mexican border. Disregard this order and we'll lay you all open to public disgrace so you'll have a time of it getting a civilian job. You could get a stretch in prison. All right, stand up to be counted!"

Ollie Spicer dropped his head in his hands and let a sob escape him. Janosek slammed his fist against a locker, then swung around and charged Bolan and was tripped up by Lew Mintzer.

"I give you my word!" Nick Ragoni said to Ben Macklin. "I never laid down. Sure, that bum liked to have me around because I was a sucker in a card game. All right, it's guilt by association, but nobody can prove I was paid a cent. Tell them to ask Arnie Cashman!"

"You know, I believe you, Nick?" Then Macklin said, "Maybe I shouldn't tell all of you this but I think you should know. Who tripped Bolan up?" He pointed with pride to Howie Patton. "As usual he took charge, men. He put two and two together and went up to the Green Hat and——"

Bolan, raging, tore at the shortstop, slipping away from Spinney's try at him, and then Howie lowered his head and slammed it into the outfielder's stomach, driving Bolan ten feet across the room and spilling him at Macklin's feet. The other players watched him struggle for breath.

Howie said, "This is the third time, Bolan. I don't want to ever lay eyes on you again."

Cy Turkin opened the door and stuck his head in. "Break it up, Ben. The writers are here."

Macklin swept his eyes over the guilty. "Anybody want to sound off to those guys? Make a statement? You'll regret it the rest of your lives if you do."

There was no answer.

"Before I forget it," Macklin said, "the boss sent you a message. 'Stick to your guns, for I haven't lost an ounce of faith in you.' " He touched his cigar off as he studied the effect. "All right, everybody suit up. I said everybody!"

The lineup Macklin brought to the plate at game time raised the eyebrows of the umpires and the Blue Sox manager.

166

PATTON	SS
ERNENWINE	LF
MINTZER	CF
SPINNEY	RF
RIKER	1B
MCIVER	C
BRAND	3B
RAGONI	2B
VILA	P

Howie, as he picked a bat from the rack, knew there was wild conjecture in the press box. He was sure the announcers on TV and radio were telling the armchair watchers that Macklin was desperate, trying any combination that would put the Gold Sox back on the winning track. They, too, were most likely admitting their amazement over the drastic reduction of power in the lineup.

The Chicago fans greeted the Little General as he walked to the plate with a rich mixture of applause and derision, and he answered it a few moments later by clubbing a pitch to the opposite field for two bases. When the Blue Sox fielder bobbled the carom off the wall, he streaked for third and slid in just ahead of the throw. From that time on it was all Gold Sox, bunting, knocking out the singles and the doubles, running crazy, with Nick Ragoni stealing some of the show from Howie. The second baseman, deeply grateful for Macklin's vote of confidence, thankful for being snatched from oblivion, slammed out three hits and stole a base.

The Gold Sox played with a fury that shook up the sixth-place Blues and had the crowd gasping for air. Felipe Vila was pitching the best game of his life, slicing the inside and outside corners of the plate with the skill of a surgeon. The Gold Sox leading, 7-0, in the seventh, Howie Patton walked with one out, raced to second on a short passed ball, tore for

167

third after tagging up on Ernenwine's fly to right, then broke for the plate when Mintzer hit a slow roller to the second baseman. The bullet throw had Howie beat but he barreled in at Wechita, the Chicago catcher, spilling him and making him drop the ball.

Wechita scrambled to his feet. He seemed about to hurl his two hundred pounds at the Gold Sox shortstop, and half a dozen of the Gold Sox came to the dugout steps. But the big catcher suddenly calmed down, picked up his mask, and went back to work.

Howie gave certain faces in the dugout a quick glance and felt a little sick inside. Men like Lubec, Steckman, and Janosek, finished at the age of thirty. Spicer, all hope gone, even for a coach's job. They sat like figures in a wax museum, no doubt picturing the drab years ahead, wondering how they had gone sour. Bolan sat with his head down as if he could not find the strength to lift it. The little shortstop tried to feel a modicum of sympathy for the towhead, but failed. Ernie Bolan had already had three chances.

13

THE GOLD SOX SWEPT IN AND OUT OF WASHING-ton, beating the Solons three straight, while the Moguls hit a snag against tight Detroit pitching and lost two, their lead cut to six games. Now the fans all over the land were talking about Howie Patton's 71 stolen bases with a month yet to go. The T-men of the Moguls, one hundred homers between them, had become little more than a matter of fact.

When the Gold Sox returned home on September 2nd to begin a series with the Blue Sox, Ollie Spicer was allowed by Macklin and the Cleveland front office to announce his retirement from baseball, ostensibly because of his health, two days after Leggett's office had accepted general Manager Engel's resignation. Writers stormed the Gold Sox clubhouse the moment Ben Macklin's presence was known at the ball park, and Garvin threw the first question. "What's going on, Ben? The public has a right to know."

"In due time," the manager hedged. "You should know the Gold Sox don't do things according to the book."

"We got a statement from Burridge after the meeting this morning, Ben. He said most of the business transacted was about allowing the two proposed National League clubs for next year to set up farm systems in advance of their impending debuts and file a reserve list. We think there was more to it than that."

"There's no law against the press thinking, friend," Macklin said, grinning. "Sometimes, though, I wish there was."

Ed Lubec came in with Mike Janosek, and three of the writers moved in on them. "I haven't a thing to say," Lubec snapped, shouldering his way past the scribes. Howie watched Lubec, and although the ex-Mogul had never been too friendly toward him, he just couldn't make himself believe this man was from the same mold as Ernie Bolan. He'd never seen anything suspicious about his actions on the ball field. Sullen at times, yes, because he'd never been given the green light often enough to swing so as to prove to the New York club they had thrown real power away. It had stuck in his craw, and he had not been able to swallow it.

Macklin waved the hesitant and muttering press toward the exit. "Clear out and let my men suit up. We've got a ball game tonight."

Ten minutes later, after making certain stubborn writers were not lingering outside, Macklin raised both hands, signaling to be heard. "After breakfast this morning, Ernie Bolan came to my suite and did a decent thing, something that might give him back a little of his self respect. He retracted certain statements, admitted he'd falsely accused Ed Lubec and Mike Janosek. They were simply suckers for an agitator who tried to sabotage Leggett. He has put it in writing and has sworn to it, and it should be in the hands of the commissioner tomorrow. There is no doubt that Ed's and Mike's cases will be reviewed."

"I fell for Bolan's line, I admit it," Janosek said, almost in tears. "But I never in my life tossed away a ball game."

Lubec said, "I didn't give you my best. I kept thinking about the Moguls and the Series check a guy with a wife and three kids sure can use and—well, I was just a louse, Ben."

"No, a knucklehead, Ed," Howie said, laughing. "We're going to *get* a Series check."

170

"Well, Steckman took us off the hook," Macklin said. "You know, he threatened to quit baseball last year because of his fear of flying. Well, he gave the writers a statement to that effect this morning before he packed up and left town." He started toward his office, stopped, and turned back. "This ought to teach all of you a good lesson about keeping your noses clean. All birds look alike if they flock together long enough. I'm sorry for my snap judgment of a few of you, but you asked for it."

When Macklin shut the door behind him, Howie said seriously, "I've known Ernie Bolan longer than any of you. When he goes to bat for anybody with nothing to gain by it, you can be sure he's telling the truth. Well, it's water under the bridge as far as I'm concerned. Any of you want to cast the first stone?"

The faces of the still subdued Lubec and Janosek lit up. "I don't deserve a break from the commish," Lubec said, "but if I get it I'll make it pay off for Macklin!"

The Gold Sox talked it up all the way from the clubhouse to the dugout. When Bert Kahl took the mound against the Blue Sox, Howie's shrill voice could be heard above the fans' steady wash of sound. The majority of the over forty thousand fans in the stadium had their eyes on him, already yelling for him to make number seventy-two. A full-throated roar spilled out over the lake when he knocked down a vicious drive by the Chicago leadoff man and threw him out at first. Bert Kahl bore down and struck out the next two hitters, and the chant began as the home team scampered off the field: "Go, Gold Sox! Go, Patton!"

The little shortstop fouled off the first pitch, taking a good cut, let two bad ones go by, then shortened up and bunted. It had too much roll on it and Holmann, the Chicago southpaw, had time to scoop it up and throw him out by a step. Stu Ernenwine drew the Blues first baseman and hot corner man in with the same bunt threat, then clubbed a single into

171

short right. Howie yelled out at Mintzer, "Get a good one, Lew. Give 'em one with eyes!" He gave Holmann a going over and needled the Chicago catcher about the excess weight he was carrying. "Don't go near the stockyards, Dobie, or they'll grab you for the lard you're packing!" he yelled.

Mintzer hung in at the plate and ran the count full, then swung at a fast ball and drove it into the left-field corner. Ernenwine, running with the pitch, never stopped until he was ten feet from the plate. He hit the dirt and slid in under Dobie's tag, Mintzer taking third. Wes Spinney's fly was caught in shallow center, and the fans came up off their seats when Mintzer tagged up and raced for the plate.

"He's a dead duck!" Nick Ragoni groaned, a fraction of a second before the ball banged into Dobie's mitt, and then Mintzer was part of a tangle of arms and legs and no out or safe sign came from the umpire until the man in blue saw the ball trickling free of the pileup. The racket in the Gold Sox dugout broke off suddenly when Mintzer failed to get to his feet. He lifted himself by the heels of his hands, turned a twisted face toward the dugout, then keeled over again. Tom Donohue ran out just ahead of Ben Macklin.

Howie, his face pale, got to the top step of the dugout, seeing himself out there in the dirt. A few moments later he heard Macklin call for a stretcher and the cold sweat came out on him as he watched them carry Mintzer off. The Gold Sox skipper picked up Willie Fairbrother with his eyes when play was about to resume once more. "You take over in center." he said soberly.

"How bad, Ben?" Lubec asked.

"A busted leg," Macklin said, then cupped his hands and yelled out at Wes Spinney. The ex-Mogul danced out of the way of a low pitch, then timed a curve and ripped it through the hole in right center for three bases. The relay from the outfield got away from the Chicago second baseman, and Spinney tore for home. The throw from the shortstop who had

172

retrieved the ball was just too late to cut off the run. Spinney grinned wide at Macklin's question, "Where did you get the wheels, Wes?" when he reached the bench.

"Guess it's contagious, Ben," the outfielder said, still short of breath. Howie was sure Ed Lubec looked a foot taller when the ex-Mogul slapped Spinney on the seat of the pants as the player headed for the drinking fountain. Remembering many things as Riker was at bat, Howie felt great satisfaction. Ever since the first time he'd put on a Little League uniform he had taken all kinds of abuse regarding his limited stature, his lack of power, but now he'd done something he swore he'd do so long ago. He'd made some very big men feel mighty small, both on and off the playing field. His "wheels" were taking a lot of attention away from the annual home-run derby and the success of ex-Argonauts like Ernenwine, Brand, Riker and the others added to his gratification.

His head snapped up when Vic Riker beat out a slow roller and took second on a low throw to first, and he yelled out to Riker to keep the wheels going around. McIver, the big catcher, got Holmann out when he drew a base on balls. Alex Brand greeted the relief man with a drag bunt and beat it out, and Nick Ragoni came up with the bases loaded. The gleeful fans yelled, "Go! Go, Gold Sox!"

Ragoni took a called strike, leaned back from an evident duster, then punched a Texas Leaguer over second that dropped between the Blue Sox center fielder and second baseman. Riker and McIver raced in to score as the fielders collided, and Nick Ragoni slid into third ahead of a desperate throw.

Howie went out to the on-deck circle, the big crowd imploring Bert Kahl to keep the big inning alive so that the little shortstop would get a cut. The pitcher, however, took three healthy swings, threw his bat away, and walked out to the mound.

While Kahl threw a few warmups to McIver, Howie took

a look at the big scoreboard, then grinned over at Alex Brand. The Oaks had scored three runs in their half of the first inning in New York. His face quickly lengthened as he thought of the four-game series coming up in the Moguls' stadium, with Lew Mintzer through for the season and Lubec's status still very much in doubt. The commissioner, they said, could be very tough sometimes, and had a heart about as soft as an umpire's.

The score did not change until the fifth. Ossatti, the Chicago slugger, connected off Kahl and hit a homer into the right-field stands that drew a hearty roar from the fans. It was only a zephyr of sound compared to the ovation Howie Patton received when he stole second in the bottom of the same inning. "Seventy-two!" the big crowd shouted in unison as Howie banged dirt off his flannels. A few moments later the spectators were standing and howling to the sky when the Gold Sox speed merchant caught the Blue Sox pitcher in a windup and stole third. He came in to score on a fielder's choice and he tipped his cap to the tremendous applause and pulsating cry, "Seventy-three! Seventy-three!"

Wes Spinney, on fire with the bat, tripled to left center and scored when Vic Riker backed the Chicago right fielder against the barrier to haul down his long fly. After the third Chicago pitcher got McIver to pop up, he walked slowly off the hill, shaking his head.

Howie checked the scoreboard when he took the field again. At the end of three innings the Oaks were leading the Moguls, 5-1. Right now Sam McCloud was very much in his mind, and he considered the many reasons why men hung on desperately when all hope seemed gone, some of them, like McCloud's, difficult for the practical mind to understand.

The last card from him had said, "Keep running, Howie. The only medicine I need you can get for me in New York." Many people have a fixed idea they live with for most of their

174

lives that is often called an obsession. In most cases it is a dream they hope may come true even though the results would not add one cent to their fortunes or their future. Howie's mother had told him on the phone, less than a week ago, "Sam's a very sick man, Howie, and I think it'll be the end of him if your team doesn't win the pennant. I can't see why baseball can be so important as it seems to be to a lot of people. They worry less, it seems to me, over the threat of the H-bomb."

He'd had to laugh a little. "Well, Mom," he said, "that's what's in Sam's mind. He wants to find out if we have a chance against the big blast. I mean, if we can beat out the Moguls."

She'd said it all sounded pretty silly to her, but he told her his dad would understand.

Bert Kahl kept mowing the visitors down until the ninth, when he got into what promised to be bad trouble. Two men were on with only one out when the Blue Sox slugger, Al Marsik, stepped in. The muscle man hit a one and two pitch to right center, a vicious drive that kept gaining height and labeled for at least three bases, but Willie Fairbrother never gave up on it and gloved it inches from the grass before tumbling over and over. From a prone position he flipped the ball to Wes Spinney, who fired to Ragoni. The second baseman threw a strike to Vic Riker, catching a Blue Sox base runner trying to get back to first, and the game was over.

In the clubhouse the writers lost no time throwing a wet blanket over the high spirits of the Gold Sox. They were less than optimistic over the chances of Macklin's team to overhaul the Moguls, even though they had cut the New York lead to five games.

"It's a pattern," a visiting scribe said. "Year after year a contender threatens the Moguls up to the last few weeks, then —pow! They take the crucial series when they have to."

"There's an end to everything," Macklin snapped angrily.

"This is a team that won't choke up, mister. We'll have more than their pitchers throwing crazy. I've been reading Hasler's pop-offs in the papers, and they're sillier than some of the comic strips."

"Up to now they've hit one hundred eighty-six homers as a club," Garvin said.

"How many down their two-hundred-ninety-seven-foot foul line?" the manager countered. "And how many stolen bases have they got?"

Ed Lubec laughed. "You watch what Hasler does if we win even half those games in New York. He'll push the panic button and call up another long bomb man from the Bees. Anybody with a village idiot's brain could win with that ball club."

"Most years," Howie remarked, as Donohue treated a slide burn on his left hip. "Not this one, Ed."

"Those players, Ben," Garvin said, "Spicer, Bolan, and Steckman. Everybody in the trade is pretty certain they quit because Leggett's type of play cramped their style."

"They can believe that if they want to." The manager grinned and lifted a cigar from the writer's handkerchief pocket. "Thanks. Havana, huh? They must pay you well."

"You must be wondering why I'm riding the bench, you guys," Lubec told the press, as he pulled on a sports shirt. "I'm allergic to fescue. That's a type of grass they put in the outfield here. I break out in a rash. I'm waiting for the groundkeepers to pull it all out and reseed."

"You're a funny man," Garvin snorted. "Let me guess the real reason. You're on the trading block."

"Maybe he is," Ben Macklin said, "but I wouldn't print it, boys. Your predictions for that series in New York will backfire on you enough. Wasn't it you, Garvin, who said the old club, the Oaks now, would finish far ahead of us? Where are they now, seventh?"

The Gold Sox, most of them ready for the street and the

break-through at the players' gate, practically laughed the scribes out of the dressing room. Macklin called out, "Check your pockets, Garvin. Howie Patton might have stolen your watch!"

It was Howie's turn to cook breakfast in the morning. When the eggs were ready he yelled at Ernenwine, still in the sack, "Come and get it!" then went out into the hall to pick up the morning paper. On the sports page he glanced at a picture of himself stealing third, read a stick of Garvin's column warning the Cleveland fans not to be optimistic about ordering Series tickets, then let his eyes rove elsewhere over the page. Suddenly they widened, and a big smile spread over his face.

Stu Ernenwine asked with a lift of his brows, "Somebody shoot a Mogul pitcher?"

"Listen to this, Stu. 'Ed Kirn, .298 hitting outfielder for the Tacoma Traders, has been brought up by the Boston Bean-eaters. Kirn, well past thirty, will be used mostly in a pinch-hitting role.' "

"Kirn? So who's Kirn?"

"I played with him in Class D, with Three Falls, Stu." The shortstop tossed his paper aside and stared up at the ceiling. "This doesn't make the game of baseball seem so rugged as guys say it is. There's always a chance if you don't stop thinking so. Like Ed told me once, you do that and you're dead. Ever stop to think how many people are needed to put you where you want to go? A kick in the slats here, a pat on the back there, a word or two of advice, and a grin when you need it?"

"No," Ernenwine said, peering curiously at the little short-stop. "Most people don't, but I guess it's a good idea. But do me a favor, Howie. Put nice thoughts out of your mind until the pennant race is over. Forget the milk of human kindness until we've licked the Moguls. You're Little Blood and Guts, remember? No quarter given, none asked."

177

Howie grinned. "When you see me getting soft, Stu, mention the Moguls. Or Arnie Cashman and the others."

"You can bet on it," Ernenwine said. "But I don't think I'll have to. Just get hold of last night's *News-Ledger* and see what Digger Lowney said for the wire services. 'I'll eat my catcher's mitt if he steals more than one base on me the entire series.' That's what the man said. He means you."

Howie went to the couch and stretched out. "Once I heard a man say that, individually, the Moguls were a pretty nice bunch, but as a team they looked down their noses at the rest of the baseball world."

"Yeah," Ernenwine said. "I wonder if an old catcher's mitt tastes good with mustard. Forget the Moguls and see what we can catch at the movies this afternoon."

Howie looked over the theatrical page of the morning paper for a few moments, then grinned at Ernenwine. "A comedy at the Strand, 'Homer's Reward,' and at the Metro, 'Bomber's Moon.' Which will it be to take our mind off baseball and the Moguls?"

178

14

THE UNBELIEVABLE GOLD SOX MOVED TO BOSTON
with a seven-game winning streak, four games behind the
Moguls. The Hub fans jammed Fenway Park to see Howie
Patton, amazing pilferer of seventy-five stolen bases, and the
brand of baseball the experts scoffed at in April. Larry Dru
and Al Burk had thirty-one mound wins between them, and
Nick Ragoni was leading the American league in number of
hits. Boston writers mentioned that Ragoni was hitting .294,
nearly twenty points better than Trafton, the New York home-
run clouter, and that "Little Blood and Guts" was not far behind his teammate, Ragoni, with .291.

In the visitors' dressing room at Fenway, Ed Lubec and
Mike Janosek clearly betrayed the strain of sitting on the edge
of a powder keg. No word had come from the commissioner.
"I guess our heads have dropped," Lubec said under his
breath to Macklin, as he hung up his coat in a locker. "And
they're pitching my 'cousin' tonight, Ben."

"The commissioner is a busy man, Ed," the manager said.
He checked the fitness of the players with the trainer. The campaign was beginning to take its toll of pulled muscles, bone
bruises, and sprains. Alex Brand was getting his ankle taped,
and Ernenwine was on his stomach on the table waiting for

Donohue to rub the oil of wintergreen on a Charley horse he'd sustained in the last ball game. Macklin examined the slide burn on Howie's thigh, making certain it had been treated with a one per cent mercurochrome solution, and only a thin layer of gauze put over it.

"It's O.K.," the little shortstop said. "It hardly bothers me at all."

At eight o'clock the Boston fans gave Howie a rousing welcome when he came up to lead off against Phil Baquette, the Beaneaters' top pitcher with a 13-11 average. The shortstop took a long look into the home dugout before he stepped into the batter's box, hoping to spot Ed Kirn, but all the hostile faces there with jaws wagging seemed very much alike. It was possible that Ed was still en route.

A note of disappointment seemed to slice through the noise of the crowd when Howie popped up to the Boston first baseman, but Ernenwine livened them up by beating out a hit to deep short. Willie Fairbrother had two strikes on him when Ernenwine took off for second and Howie knew his roommate was a dead pigeon before he was halfway to the pick-up station. The Boston fans began to jeer and hoot when Ernenwine picked himself up and trotted to the dugout. Willie Fairbrother looked at a third strike, and the Gold Sox took the field.

Felipe Vila set the Beaneaters down in order and the game turned into a pitcher's battle. At the end of five there were only goose eggs on the scoreboard. The fans taunted Howie when he led off in the top of the sixth. He'd struck out his second time at bat. Baquette worked on him carefully, trying to keep the ball high to reduce the possibility of a good bunt. With the count two balls and two strikes, the Boston first and third basemen moved in, and Howie rammed a single over the hot corner man's head. Turning first, he saw the Boston left fielder bobble the ball for a few seconds, and he kept running. The throw came in and he slid into the bag on his stomach, the umpire immediately giving the safe sign.

From second Howie yelled, "Pick me up, Stu!" and took a long lead.

Ernenwine took a good cut at Baquette's first pitch, shortened up, and bunted the pitcher's second offering up the first-base line, sacrificing Howie to third. Willie Fairbrother hit a long foul into the left-field seats, then cut hard and missed on a change-up. Howie looked out at the Boston fielders, then shifted his glance to Macklin in the dugout. The fans and the Beaneater defense were dead certain that the hitter was after the fly ball that would bring in a big Gold Sox run. Fairbrother refused to bite at a curve outside, got out, and rubbed dirt on his hands. He looked as if he were making ready to murder the ball when he got back in and dug his spikes in deep. Baquette fired and Fairbrother quickly dumped the ball between the mound and first base, with Howie on the run. There was no chance to beat the squeeze, and Baquette just got Fairbrother by a half step. Vic Riker got the green light to hit away and lined out to the Boston shortstop.

The Beaneaters' power hitter, Sam Ruffner, tied the ball game up in the seventh with a long blast over the screen in left, and the Boston rooters wildly cheered him as he touched all the bases. Shaken by the blast, Vila walked the next two men. Howie ran in and talked to him, the fans hooting at the little shortstop. Macklin came out and asked the Puerto Rican if he wanted to stay in and Vila said, "Ees hokay, skipper." When Howie returned to his position at short he saw that the Boston second baseman was being called back to the bench. The announcer's voice blared out of the P.A. system.

"Batting for Descher, number thirty-seven. Ed Kirn!"

Howie watched Ed come out of the Boston dugout swinging three bats, and suddenly he felt good inside. When Kirn got set to hit, however, he became a stranger to him, an enemy

181

determined to upset his applecart. He yelled in at the pinch hitter, "When did you get out of the old men's home, Kirn?"

The batter stepped out and leveled a puzzled glance at the Gold Sox shortstop. He grinned when he stepped back in. Vila had to fire eight pitches before Kirn lined out deep to Fairbrother, the runners advancing. Howie grinned at the dirt at his feet. Ed sure had put good wood to the ball. A few moments later he raced to his left, backhanded a drive that seemed about to go through the hole, and flipped the ball to Alex Brand to end the Boston threat.

With one out in the ninth, Howie missed a bunt attempt, chopped a foul to the right of the plate, and had the Boston infield shuttling in and out. Baquette worked him too fine and ran the count even, the capacity crowd calling for a strikeout.

He checked the sign, found he was still on his own, and when Baquette turned loose a half speed curve he choked up on the thick handle of his bat and blooped the ball into short right. He took a wide turn at first, then scampered back, the spectators in an uproar. He drew two throws with Ernenwine at bat, then took off when the Boston catcher had to lunge for a pitch low and inside. He slid into second with time to spare but got up in a hurry when the ball bounced off his protective helmet and rolled toward right field. He reached third standing up, and Cy Turkin called for time to ask him how he was.

"Had bees in my head for a few seconds, Cy," Howie said. "That's all."

The partisan crowd had seen what it had come to see, the amazing running of the Little General and his seventy-sixth stolen base, and it seemed to forget that Phil Baquette was well on his way to losing the ball game. Ernenwine swung away and popped up to the Boston catcher, and now the fans started buzzing, wondering if this crazy Gold Sox team would try a squeeze again. Baquette kept the ball high on the Cleveland left-fielder, and with the count three balls and one strike he

182

tried to cut the inside corner of the plate. The ball was low and into the dirt and the Boston catcher partially blocked it. Howie Patton raced in when the ball rolled only a few feet away from the plate, and he slid in under the lunging Beaneater receiver, rolling the man over on his back.

The umpire called the runner safe, and the Boston manager stormed out of the dugout. Baquette moved in and kicked dirt on the ump's trousers and was immediately put out of the game. Howie was grinning when he reached the dugout, and Fenway Park was jumping, the fans calling for umpire blood.

The Gold Sox held on and took a 2-1 win into the dressing room. "A real tough one," Spinney said, drawing a deep breath.

"They'll all be as rough, the rest of the way in," Macklin said, and made his way toward his shortstop. A bruise was beginning to swell on Howie's cheekbone where the Boston catcher's knee had hit. "I wish I knew what you were made of, kid," the manager said. "I'd order a few carloads." He moved to where Donohue was unwinding the tape on Alex Brand's ankle. He caught a look of pain in the third baseman's eyes and knew the ex-Argonaut needed a few days' rest. Tomorrow he'd have to put Cortena at the hot corner.

The word came in that the Moguls had swamped the Bluejays, 12-5, Trafton and Torkl hitting for the circuit, and Howie felt a moment of deep misgiving. Time was running out.

When the players filled the dressing room the next night, they found Macklin wearing a big smile. The manager announced that Lubec and Janosek were in the clear. "They'll play tonight. At the same time, I'm fining them both a hundred and fifty dollars for the wear and tear they put on me, and for breaking club rules!"

"It'll be a pleasure, Ben," Lubec said and hooked an arm around Mike Janosek's neck and drew him to him. "If you want the big bunt, Ben, just let me know."

183

The Gold Sox, at full strength again, went out and beat Boston, 8-2, Frank Delmar hurling a six hitter. Lubec, reborn, hit a single and a double. Janosek stole a base and clubbed a triple. Howie's contribution was three walks that turned into two runs. The baseball deities were also kind this night, for they saw to it that the Baltimore club won a 6-5 extra-inning game from the Moguls.

"Three games behind," Macklin said, when he let the writers in. "Who pitches tomorrow? It'll be Kahl, boys. I want Dru and Burk ready for the Moguls."

"I think Hasler's a little spooky," a Boston *Record-Telegram* writer said. "He hasn't made a statement for two days."

As usual, the scribes crowded around the Gold Sox spark plug, drawing little personal details out of him, asking him what he thought his total number of stolen bases would be after 162 games. Was there a girl somewhere and what did his father do? Had he an agent yet to get him on TV and into the ads?

"I've been approached by agents," Howie said. "I don't ever intend to say I go for anything I don't really believe in. Some of those endorsements are as phony as Chinese home runs."

"Now I've heard everything," a writer said, shaking his head.

The next afternoon, under a hot sun, Bert Kahl put on a certain pair of his thick-lensed specs and pitched the Gold Sox's tenth straight victory, 3-2. Macklin let Lubec swing away in the sixth, and the center fielder put it over the screen in left with Ernenwine aboard. A message came to Howie after he'd showered. It was from Ed Kirn. "How big a little guy has become!" the Boston player had scribbled. "Too big to go hunting with an old bush leaguer when the season's over?"

Howie said under his breath, as he crumpled the message up and shoved it into his pocket, "It's a date, Ed."

Tomorrow was an open date. The road secretary gave the

184

players the time they were to be at the South Station for the train ride to New York. At the moment, the standing of the three top teams in the league was:

	WON	LOST	
MOGULS	95	45	.679
GOLD SOX	92	48	.657
BENGALS	82	59	.581

Up to now the two contenders had split the fourteen games they'd played. The majority of the baseball fans all over the country were forgetting fallout, high taxes and creeping inflation. In New York, soon, they'd find out whether or not small arms could stand up against the long-range missile and the big bomb, whether Gold Sox speed and finesse could win out over Mogul power. The tension began to take hold of Howie and Stu Ernenwine the next morning. They caught themselves being short with each other after breakfast, particularly when they'd read the morning papers. The experts doubted that the Gold Sox could more than break even in the four-game set. Moreover, a team with a ten-straight streak was due to be brought up with a jolt. The Gold Sox had to sweep to stay in serious contention. They would face Kroll, the crafty southpaw, in the opener, and the pitcher had a 19-3 record thus far.

"We beat *him*," Ernenwine said, "and it'll be like the first hard punch in a prize fight." He fired the newspaper half across the room. "Let's take a walk and forget we're ballplayers."

Howie picked up some mail at the desk, including a card postmarked Hagersville, Vermont. Sam McCloud's handwriting seemed steadier. It told the shortstop, *You guys can do it. I'm not supposed to be watching on TV because the doc says the excitement might be too much for me. Who's he kidding, Howie? Run them ragged, kid!*

He felt better. Maybe the medicine Sam McCloud needed

185

was in New York, the ingredients of the prescription a pair of incredibly fast legs, an educated bat, determination, and plenty of grit, most generally known in the trade as guts. Stuffing the rest of the mail into his pocket, he said, "We'll take the Moguls, Stu."

Ernenwine grinned. "Sure. Let's find a cemetery, Howie. As we pass by we'll whistle as loud as we can."

Nearly sixty thousand people were in the Mogul stadium on Friday night, clamoring for the umpires to come out and get the game underway. It was hot and humid, and millions of insects swarmed in the glare of the light towers. Howie, never more anxious to break the leash, walked up and down in front of the bat rack, amazed at his lack of nerves. Macklin went out with his lineup, and Howie watched George Hasler leave the home dugout and approach the plate on slightly bowed legs. The Mogul manager was well over sixty-five.

"Get on," Lubec was already telling the little shortstop. "Start us off good."

The field cleared and a great roar welled up and steadily rose in volume as the Moguls raced out onto the field. Rusty Kroll strode to the mound. Then the big crowd welcomed Howie Patton back to the stadium with a thunderous burst of applause, proving that exceptional talent was appreciated everywhere, even in the lair of the Moguls. When he dug in at the plate, however, the thousands of fans implored Kroll to get him out. The unpolished ones loudly advised the southpaw to stick the ball right in the batter's ear.

"This is as far as you hot-shots go," Digger Lowney growled, when Howie looked at a strike. "We're separatin' ourselves from the boys this series."

"That mitt don't look very edible," Howie shot back. He made as if to bunt, but pulled back in time when the pitch sailed outside. Lowney kept up his verbal jabbing. He laughed when Kroll backed Howie away with a pitch designed to

186

"make him honest." The count was all the way out when he clubbed a change-up to the ground six feet in front of the plate that turned into a Baltimore chop. Before the ball came down into the shortstop's glove he was making the turn at first, and Gold Sox fans throughout the stands screamed for Howie to go.

He tantalized Kroll with long leads, evaded two of the south-paw's famous pick-off throws with stomach slides while Ern-enwine was hitting, then brought wrath down upon his head when he spilled Shillaber, the Mogul shortstop, trying for a double play when Ernenwine forced him at second. Kroll ended the mild threat by striking out both Lubec and Vic Riker, and the Mogul fans relaxed, refilling their lungs in case the New York lightning struck early.

With Howie talking it up behind him, Larry Dru struck out the first two men to face him, then got Torkl, one of the T-men, to fly to Spinney in right. Along with Kroll he kept nothing but ciphers on the scoreboard through the fourth inning, but in the last of the fifth, Jumbo Hauser, the New York first baseman, got hold of a fast ball and rode it into the second tier of the stands in right, and Mogul rooters made full use of their time to howl. The one run kept assuming mammoth proportions when Kroll began the seventh by strik-ing out Nick Ragoni. He struck out Larry Dru. The Mogul rooters were shouting, "Bye-bye, Gold Sox." They jeered Howie Patton when he stepped in for his third official time at bat.

The little shortstop turned a deaf ear to Digger Lowney's ribbing and thought of Sam McCloud, who would be watching. He liked Kroll's first pitch and quickly dumped it up the first-base line. He seemed to have been running even as the bat met the ball. He reached first without drawing a throw and Hauser came in to hold him on. "This is the end of the line, Little General," he said, out of the corner of his mouth.

"Not when I hold a ticket to the next stop, Jumbo," Howie

187

said, and a few seconds later when Kroll threw his first pitch to Ernenwine he took off at full speed for the middle sack, barreled into it with a hook slide, and evaded the tag. He grinned as he heard Cass McIver's voice come out of the dugout. "That's *the* one, Digger! You want the mitt with catsup or French dressin'?"

Stu Ernenwine looked up the line at Cy Turkin and then stepped back in to hit. He worked Kroll for a ball, took a called strike, and then fouled seven pitches off. The southpaw looked back at second, suddenly whirled, and threw as his shortstop cut in behind the base runner. The ball went wild and Howie streaked for third. Shaken, Kroll walked the Gold Sox left fielder, and then Ed Lubec, still deeply grateful to Macklin for his second chance, poked the first pitch that came to him between center and left for a triple, driving in Howie and Ernenwine to put the Gold Sox out in front, 2-1.

Hasler lost no time coming out to the mound and signaling to the bullpen for a fireman. Tom Aber, veteran relief man, took the long walk in with Vic Riker waiting at the plate. The Gold Sox bench kept lacing it into Digger Lowney, who was out on the hill with Hasler, and they ribbed Kroll when he walked toward the Mogul dugout. Aber had a knuckler that did tricks and he retired Riker on four pitches. The fans settled back, hoping for the eruption of Mogul power that very often came in the last two innings.

Larry Dru, his fast ball still alive and well under control, left the mound in the last of the eighth, still holding the one-run lead. First man up for the Gold Sox, he waved futilely at Aber's stuff and said to Howie, as he walked back to the dugout, "Get me an insurance run."

Aber threw a slow curve that failed to get a corner. He fired a knuckler that was in on Howie's chin, then threw a pitch high and outside. A second knuckler was called a strike, but he lost the Gold Sox flyer with his fourth pitch, one that

188

turned Lowney around to jaw at the umpire. The fans were on the edges of their seats again, yelling at the base runner, daring him to go. Howie had a long lead when Ernenwine cracked Aber's second pitch to right field. Torkl got the drive on one hop and fired to third, failing to get Howie as he slid in.

Lubec, as he dug in at the plate, looked over at his old team-mates in the Mogul dugout, threw impolite remarks their way, then took his widespread stance and looked out at Aber. He cut at the first pitch and skied deep to left, and Howie tagged up and trotted in with the third run for Cleveland. Crossing the plate he laughed at Digger Lowney. "What else is new?" he asked the steaming catcher.

Very few spectators were leaving the stands when Vic Riker struck out. The big crowd called for the rally when the Moguls came in to swing. It would be the wrecking crew, Torkl, Trafton, Lowney and Hauser. The blood cry pyramided when Torkl pulled a vicious drive into right that bounced into the stands for a ground-rule double, and Mitch Moger stepped up his firing in the visitor's bullpen. Howie came in, along with Riker, to talk to Larry Dru, and Cass McIver joined the hud-dle. Dru said, "If you think I'm losing this one, you guys, you're out of your cotton-pickin' minds."

The umpire broke up the summit meeting and then Larry Dru, his uniform soaked in sweat, reared back and struck the great Trafton out with just four pitches. Tormented by the barrage from the Gold Sox bench, Digger Lowney finally popped up to Ragoni; he nearly took the legs out from under the New York third-base coach when he threw his war club away. The fans implored Jumbo Hauser to hit the long bomb. Larry Dru made the big first baseman wait, then gave him a blazing fast ball in tight that cut the inside corner. He threw one low and outside that the overanxious swinger cut at and missed, then gave Hauser a big motion and pulled the string.

189

The hitter swung, disturbing nothing but the night air, and the ball game was over.

The Gold Sox players swarmed in and over Larry Dru, pounding him on about every portion of his anatomy save his pitching arm. They reached for his hand and they hugged him. Thousands in the stands seemed to be taking their time moving toward the exits, as if what they had seen had stunned them for a few moments. The first pill for Sam McCloud, Howie thought, as he made his way to the dressing room.

Much of the Gold Sox exuberance had worn off as the players peeled off their sodden flannels. It had been a tough one to win, and there were three more left. Tomorrow afternoon it would be Steen for the Moguls, and he'd beaten them his last two starts against them.

"Get your seventy-eighth tomorrow, Howie," Wes Spinney said. "We've got the bottle of mustard for Digger."

15

THE FANS TURNED OUT IN GREAT NUMBERS THE following afternoon, under a hot and sultry sky. Ben Macklin pulled a surprise move at the last minute that had Hasler shuffling his batting order. Felipe Vila was going to the mound instead of Al Burk. That morning the southpaw had sought out Macklin and had said, "Let me peetch, si? Las' night I have dream an' San Rafael comes to me an' says *mañana,* tomorrow ees your day, Felipe. Si, my birthday."

At the end of the first inning, Ben Macklin regretted following the hunch. Two runs were over for the Moguls before Vila got the side out. When the pitcher came in, he had not lost his big smile. "Eet ees hokay," he assured the manager. "Don' you worry one leetle beet."

Steen kept containing the Gold Sox, giving up but one hit through four innings and walking but one man, Howie Patton. Felipe Vila, a fair hitting pitcher, led off in the first of the fifth with the big New York crowd happy and in full voice. Howie knelt in the batter's box, yelling encouragement to Felipe, who responded by lining a single through the hole between third and short. The fans got on Howie when he stepped in, along with Digger Lowney and the entire Mogul bench. He thought of the picture of himself on a television screen in Vermont, then hit Steen's first pitch off the thick handle of his bat and dropped it into short center. Hasler came to the top step of his dugout, waving to his bullpen.

Ernenwine made Steen work, then rode a pitch to right field, and Vila tagged up and raced to third, sliding in ahead of a good throw from the Moguls' Trafton. The attempt to get the front runner backfired, Howie Patton steaming into second. On the mound, Steen took a long deep breath and then pitched to Ed Lubec, missing with his first two offerings. Hasler ordered Lubec walked with first base open, gambling on the double play.

Steen, his infield in double-play depth, brought a delighted roar from the fans when he struck out Vic Riker, and Howie, leading off second, cupped his hands over his mouth and yelled in at Wes Spinny, digging in against Steen, "Just a small hit, Wes! The old-fashioned single!"

The Mogul right-hander threw two quick strikes past Spinney. With the thousands of rooters confident that the threat was stopped, it came to his mind that the batter expected a waste pitch here and would watch a good one go by. He turned one loose down the middle, but Spinney's bat came around easily, just meeting the ball. It was a clothesline a foot inside the left-field foul line, which the Mogul left fielder had to chase to the corner. Vila and Howie scored, and Spinney reached second standing up.

The noise in the stadium was suddenly reduced to a minimum. Hasler seemed about ready to lift Steen, but the pitcher got a reprieve when he got McIver out on a pop-up just outside third.

In the seventh, Trafton connected after two were out, bringing the Mogul rooters fully alive, but Felipe Vila just looked in at Macklin, flashed his white teeth, and proceeded to strike out Digger Lowney. Steen, buoyed up by the long bomb, retired Janosek, Ragoni, and Vila in the top of the

192

eighth, and Macklin's southpaw returned the compliment in the bottom half.

The Gold Sox came in to hit with three outs left to them. Nearly sixty thousand rabid rooters pressured Howie Patton when he walked toward the plate. Looking out at Steen, it occurred to him that the pitcher felt some strain himself. In the eighth he'd been getting his first pitch over, getting ahead of the hitters. Steen's first pitch did come over, just around the knees, and quickly Howie shortened up and dumped the ball down the third-base line. As he put his head down and raced to first, he was sure he'd hit a little too hard and would never make it, but a sudden roar of dismay from the stands told him that Petrie, the Mogul third baseman, must have lost the handle on the ball. Crossing first, he looked over his shoulder, and saw Petrie angrily slam the ball to Steen. Jumbo Hauser said a moment later, holding the runner on, "Horseshoes, you fresh little shrimp!"

"I love you, too, Jumbo. I'm sorry, but I forgot to bring you peanuts today."

The New York infield expected another bunt, for there was an old adage in baseball that said you had to tie it up before you could win it. Ernenwine faked a bunt, then swung away on Steen's second pitch and hit a single into right, and Howie Patton raced around to third, the fans marveling at his speed. Trafton threw into second for the cutoff but Ernenwine, halfway down the line, scampered back to first. Here, Hasler came out and asked Steen for the ball, and a fireman left the Mogul bullpen. It looked like Ray Thurman to Howie.

Thurman took his seven preliminary warmups, then worked on Ed Lubec and induced him to foul out to Lowney. "You're overdue," Howie shouted out at Riker, next up, but the first baseman, after running the count to two balls and two strikes, stood and watched a good curve go by. Hasler made his move here, aware of Wes Spinney's power. He ordered Wes put on, to guard against the squeeze, for the Gold Sox catcher, up next, was no speed merchant.

Hundreds of spectators were on the move toward the runways when McIver checked the sign with Turkin. The big catcher looked a low pitch over, then the crack of his bat drove the roar of thousands back into their throats. Torkl started running, then put on the brakes and watched the ball settle into the left field seats a good ten rows back, and the Gold Sox swarmed to the dugout steps to watch the grinning McIver circle the bases behind three runners. Gold Sox, 6-3.

Felipe Vila fairly screeched, "I tol' you so, deedn't I, Mackleen?" as the Gold Sox mobbed McIver.

Macklin sleeved sweat from his face. "It's the only reason I gave him the green light," he growled. "It was a dumb move, even if it did work. Now you'd better hold 'em off, Felipe."

After Janosek made the third out, Vila strode to the mound and retired the downcast Moguls in order, and the fired-up Gold Sox ran off only a game out of first place. Running alongside Janosek, Howie said, under his breath, "How's the medicine working so far, Sam?"

The third baseman threw him a surprised glance and reminded him his name was Mike.

The newspapers the next morning said this was an unbelievable ball club, the most determined group of athletes the writers had ever seen. It was a hungry club, fully dedicated to a cause, and its running, bunting, and punch-hitting had thrown Hasler's club off balance. Howie Patton was a sensational rookie. He held the Gold Sox up and kept the fire under them. New York scribes, however, inferred that they'd still bet the old homestead and the family jewels on the Moguls' chances of bouncing back in tomorrow's doubleheader.

The stadium was packed on Sunday. Over seventy thousand people, expecting Mogul power to break out and bury the

Gold Sox at any moment, chewed their nails as Al Burk refused to weaken. The control pitcher had given up but two hits in six innings, more than matching the Mogul Caulfield's performance. Howie, leading off in the seventh, looking for his first time on base, slashed a full-count pitch toward third that bounced off Petrie's chest and rolled toward the line. The infielder pounced on it, whirled, and threw to first, a foot over Hauser's head. Howie raced to second, a note of dismay in the big crowd's steady racket.

Stu Ernenwine hit a drive that Hauser knocked down back of first and beat the Gold Sox left fielder to the bag by three steps, Howie reaching third. A desperate, imploring note crept into the Mogul rooters' hoarse throats.

Caulfield worked carefully on Lubec, trying to keep the ball low. He got ahead of his ex-teammate, nothing and two, then missed with three straight pitches. Lubec hit the payoff delivery to left field, foul by a foot. Kaufman, the Mogul fielder, raced over and plucked it out of the seats, whirled, and fired into Lowney, but Howie Patton seemed like the second stage of a rocket after he'd tagged up. He slid in as Lowney lunged to his left to get the throw, and the Gold Sox were leading, 1-0. A great sigh welled up from the spectators when Riker fanned.

The fans kept waiting, but Burk refused to lose his stuff. Twice he'd struck out Torkl; Trafton, once. He went through the eighth, into the ninth, with the slim lead. Still the loyal Mogul rooters refused to believe as he faced Petrie, the first man up for Hasler. The leadoff man had to get on. He went for the bunt, but Al Burk flagged it down fast just to the right of the mound and threw to Riker in time. The shadows were lengthening in the big stadium, along with thousands of faces, when Lou Shillaber flied out to Ernenwine. Torkl dug in at the plate, bringing Mogul fans' hopes alive.

The slugger took a terrific cut at Burk's first pitch, missed, and nearly sat down in the dirt. He shied away from one off the fists, then took another healthy cut, fouling it back against the screen. Al Burk threw again and Torkl looked at it, and the curve ball caught the outside corner for the called third strike. The Mogul slugger stood there for several moments, then turned and slowly walked away. Howie was the first man to run in and get his arms around Al Burk. He planted a kiss on the grinning pitcher's weathered cheek.

The Gold Sox were tied for the league lead.

"Get that second steal on Lowney in the nightcap, Howie!" Lubec yelled at the little shortstop, as the team moved toward the dressing room. "Lord, what a game Al pitched!"

"I agree," Ben Macklin shouted at the stripping players. "We're unbelievable. Let's stay that way!"

"The pressure is on the Moguls now," Cy Turkin yelled, and tipped a beverage can to his lips.

The coach's words were prophetic. Petrie fumbled Howie's grounder as the second game of the day got under way, and then the Mogul second baseman attempted to force Howie at second after heading off Ernenwine's ground ball just inside the skin of the infield. He missed by a good margin, and all hands were safe. Choate, Hasler's first-year sensation, threw a strike past Lubec, then wild-pitched the Gold Sox runners to second and third. Lubec swung at the next pitch and drove it straight at the shortstop, and the thousands looking on turned loose a roar of despair when Bailee tried to throw before he had a grip on the ball. It squirted away from him and Howie, having held up, raced in and scored.

After Vic Riker looked at a third strike, Wes Spinney lined a single to center, bringing in Ernenwine. Choate, aware that his manager was on the top step of the dugout, bore down and got rid of McIver and Janosek.

Mogul fans were suddenly brought out of the depths when Mogul power burst loose in the bottom of the inning. After

196

retiring the leadoff man, Bert Kahl was knocked out. Shillaber singled, and Torkl doubled him to third. Trafton rode his fifty-fifth home run into the bleachers for three runs, and Digger Lowney kept the big inning alive with a single. Vila, Macklin's fire man, struck out Hauser, but Bailee, a light hitter, kept the fans in a frenzy by tripling Lowney home. Ben Macklin, a heavy sigh escaping him, left the dugout. He called Sal Sava, a lefthander, out of the bullpen.

Sava got the third man out and the Gold Sox came in, feeling the full force of the crowd's derision. The fans seemed to be reminding the visitors that first place belonged to the Moguls and that the Gold Sox had had their last day in the sun.

The score remained 4-2, in favor of the Moguls until the fourth, and from that time on the fans in the stadium and at the television sets saw a ball game they would not forget if they all lived to be ninety. They saw Howie Patton bunt himself on, steal second while Ernenwine struck out, race to third on a fielder's choice, and then score on Lubec's scratch single to deep short. They saw Alex Brand and Mitch Moger come out onto the top step of the dugout, the third baseman waving a paper plate at Digger Lowney, and the relief pitcher holding up a big jar of mustard.

They saw Hauser hit for the circuit in the sixth with a man on, to put the home team out in front, 6-3, and then were treated to a sensational double steal by Nick Ragoni and Howie Patton in the seventh that set up a two-run inning on but one hit. They saw the announcement go up on the scoreboard, while the Moguls batted in the same inning, that said the little Gold Sox shortstop had stolen eighty bases!—the greatest total since Cobb.

The slightly insane capacity crowd took out all stops when the Moguls seemed to have the game sewed up in the seventh. They had scored another run off Sava, but Macklin's incredible team punched Choate for two hits in the eighth, after Spinney drew a walk to tie the score at seven all. The game went into the eleventh and the lights were turned on, and the spectators used what strength they had left in their lungs pleading for the big Mogul home run.

They saw Howie Patton sacrifice Ragoni to second, after Cortena, pinch-hitting, had struck out, and wrapped themselves up in gloom when Ed Lubec singled the lead run home. When the Moguls came in to hit they hoped and prayed for the long ball that never came from Mitch Moger's sharp relief pitching, and moved slowly out of the stadium wondering what kind of men these Gold Sox were who had practically run the Moguls out of first place.

They read the next morning that Digger Lowney had ripped his uniform to shreds in the clubhouse and that Jumbo Hauser threw a punch at a writer. Hasler gave them comfort, reminding them that eighteen games were still to be played. The Moguls could still finish a good five games in front.

Flying back home, the Gold Sox were glad of a two-day respite before they played a two-game set with the Bluejays. Most of the elation they'd felt over the sweep at the Mogul stadium had been left back in the dressing room. Reaction had set in; the series had been very exacting, and up ahead the second division clubs, "the spoilers," would be eager to knock them off.

Howie Patton thought of Sam McCloud. He was certain he had heard him laughing when the last out was made in New York. The first thing he would do on arrival would be to put in a call to Hagersville. He tipped his seat back and closed his eyes, recalling the things he'd read in the newspapers the past ten days. Owners were seriously considering changes in the ball parks designed to cut down the cheap home runs. . . . Howie Patton and several of Macklin's players had taken the spotlight away from the muscle men. . . . Big

198

league scouts, if the Gold Sox won the pennant, would surely turn their attention to the small but compact little players with the ability to get the hits that had "eyes," players that could run and lay down a bunt. . . . The baseball itself would undergo new tests, despite opinions of the exponents of the big blast. . . .

Being human, the little shortstop enjoyed his claim to fame, but he was far more proud of what he had done for "too small" kids, now playing in the Little Leagues or yet to be born, than he was of his eighty stolen bases. Now, a lot of them might be given the chance to display their talents. Team statistics came to his mind, and he grinned to himself. The Gold Sox had only one .300 hitter, Ed Lubec. The team average was .253, and Macklin's men had hit only 57 home runs. But they had set a record for stolen bases (162) and for number of times getting on base.

Ben Macklin passed the word the length of the DC-8. A big crowd and a brass band were waiting at the airport. Alex Brand came up out of a short nap and said after a big yawn, "They're putting the cart before the horse. If we blow it on the last road trip they'll come to meet us, too. With armfuls of rocks."

An hour later, Howie and Ernenwine reached their apartment and breathed twin sighs of utter relief. The shortstop's sports coat had been split halfway up the back, and there was a smear of rouge on his chin where a hysterical lady fan had planted a kiss. After he had assembled his marbles, he put in a call to Hagersville.

"Your dad's popped off all the buttons on his vest," his mother told him excitedly. "The whole town's talking about you! I'm so proud I just can't——"

"Sure, sure, Mom, but tell me. How is Sam McCloud?"

"He was here just an hour ago—and Howie, it just doesn't seem possible! He looked real good, and only a few weeks ago we all expected to hear at any minute that——"

Howie laughed. "I knew he'd hang in there after getting knocked down. Tell him we'll keep making the medicine."

"Whatever that means," his mother said, and put his father on.

Harry Patton admitted he was all of fifteen years late in fully appreciating the kind of son he had, and certainly realized now that if you pile up the pennies the dollars will take care of themselves. The Gold Sox were certainly proving it.

A few seconds after Howie cradled the phone, it started ringing and he snatched it up again. "Howie?" a familiar voice said. "This is Iffy. I'm back to make sure you guys don't blow it. Didn't Macklin tell you?"

"This is great, just great!" Howie shouted. "No, he didn't tell us. He likes surprises, Iffy. Ask the Moguls."

"I'm coming right over," Oldam said. "What's that address?"

Iffy Oldam got a rousing welcome in the Cleveland clubhouse just before the Gold Sox went out to play the Bluejays, and only a half hour later he thanked them all by slicing a single to right with the bases loaded, building a four-run lead for Larry Dru. Macklin's ace never let go of it despite a round-tripper with one on in the eighth by the Bluejays' pinch hitter, Sileo.

Their fifteen-game winning streak was broken the next night, but the Moguls, still a little shocked by their going-over by Macklin's club, lost to the Bengals. The Minnesota Gophers moved in for four games; Howie Patton, Oldam, Alex Brand, and Ernenwine ran crazy, and Lubec and Spinney stayed hot with their bats and won three of them. The Moguls faltered in Chicago and dropped three full games behind, and World's Series fever broke out along the shores of Lake Erie.

Trafton had to share the headlines with Howie Patton the morning after he'd hit his fifty-seventh homer. The Little

200

General had stolen his eighty-third base in the opener of a three-game set with the Kansas City Bees. Most of the writers considered Howie's feat the greatest thing that had happened to baseball during the last three decades. Already, on several ball clubs, the power hitters were shortening their swings and cutting down their number of strikeouts. Today's age is one of science and speed, and the world of baseball was beginning to recognize that fact.

"Don't make any plans for tomorrow afternoon," Macklin told the Gold Sox, as they suited up for the second game with the Bees. "All of you are to be at the Biltmore at twelve thirty, wearing ties. That's all I'll tell you now, except go out and get us another ball game."

"A tie!" Riker said. "Who's got a tie?"

Stu Ernenwine slept until nearly eleven o'clock the next morning, and Howie had to literally drag him out of the sack. Ordinarily a quick man to shower and shave, the left fielder seemed to drag both processes out. He used up nearly a half hour drinking his coffee and looking over the morning paper, and Howie began to lose his patience. "Look, knucklehead, we'll be late!" he finally yelled at the left fielder. "And it's ten to one the big boss is throwing this luncheon, or whatever it'll turn out to be."

"We've got time, Howie. Keep your sliding pads on," Ernenwine said, and held up three ties for the shortstop's inspection. "Which should I wear?"

"Put 'em all on," Howie snapped, and paced the floor. His watch said it was high noon and he ground his teeth as he thought of the traffic they'd buck getting to the hotel. He suddenly stopped and squinted at Ernenwine. "Why the silly grin on your homely face?"

They reached the hotel ten minutes late and were informed at the desk that the Leggett party was taking place in the Jade Room, just off the mezzanine. Ernenwine got behind Howie when they got there and shoved him through the door. The shortstop froze in his tracks when he saw the faces grinning at him from the ornate festive table. His jaw hung loose as Ernenwine said, "Well, I had a time stalling him, Mr. Leggett, but here he is!"

The shortstop kept staring, hardly believing. There was Herb Sayre and Jim Brentwood, Jake Pitzer, and—yes, Sam McCloud! With McCloud was Doc Hannaford, the doctor that had brought Howie into the world. McCloud's face was one big smile. Cass McIver picked up a glass and held it high. "Let's give it to him, boys!"

They sang the parody while Howie made his way to the vacant chair between Frank Leggett, multimillionaire, and Sam McCloud, ex-big league ballplayer. "For he's a pretty fast fellow! That the Moguls can't deny!"

He was hardly aware of shaking hands with the owner, or of the words of praise that came from him. The past had been brought to this room along with the three men who had been responsible for his development, and he felt the urge to let go until Macklin said laughingly, "The Gold Sox don't choke up, kid."

He swallowed hard, turned and put an arm around McCloud. "You old faker. Who were you trying to kid this time?"

Doc Hannaford said, "Believe me, Howie, he wasn't kidding. He really had two strikes on him and was ready to be waved out. He picked up all of a sudden!"

Herb Sayre called to him from across the table. "Remember Pete—Pete Rogell, Howie? He's with the Covington Colts and due to be brought up to the Blue Sox."

"We've got a new bus at Three Falls, kid," Jake Pitzer said. "It's got brakes. The old one fell apart just as we pulled into Kingston one day. Remember that beanery at——?"

202

They all talked at once while they ate the fruit cup, the filet mignons and the baked Alaska. They discussed the pitchers of the league leaders, the Chiefs, and the weaknesses of the hitters. Jim Brentwood shifted the talk to the Argonauts and ribbed Howie about a new kid he'd brought up from a Nebraska college. "I think he might be even a little faster than you, Howie."

The table was cleared and the photographers came in, armed with flashbulbs. Frank Leggett got up and thanked the Gold Sox for their terrific performance on the field and for their splendid cooperation when it seemed outside influences had wrecked a dream he'd had for many years. "This young fellow here," he said, putting a hand on Howie's shoulder, "took charge for me, and I must confess I have only paid him a minimum wage." He laughed, picked up a long official-looking envelope, and handed it to his shortstop. "Eighty-three stolen bases times a hundred, Howie. It is my pleasure to present this to you."

The Jade Room shook with applause. Players and guests stood up while Howie sat there in a kind of trance, his eyes getting much too bright. They made him get to his feet, and he said, "The money, Mr. Leggett, I like. But it can't buy the kind of guys you invited here today. I-I thank you all very much."

A long time after it was over, Howie agreed with the writers that Doc Hannaford, the old country doctor, made the most pertinent speech. "I've never held too much to this game of professional baseball and never could figure out why so many grown men followed it like it was a religion," Doc said. "To me it was just summer insanity, that might get cured in the fall by sulphur and molasses."

He waited for the laughter to subside, then gestured toward Sam McCloud.

"Since I've seen a miracle happen, I've changed my mind.

Look at this man here! Would you think he was close to the twilight zone two months ago? Now, I'll give him at least fifteen more years if he don't do somethin' foolish like takin' up the cha-cha. If baseball can do this for a man, let's make sure it's played for at least a thousand more years. It must be a way of life. The first thing I do when I get back home is learn how to figure out a box score."

"We've got nine games left," Macklin said, when all the others had had their licks, "after we beat the Bees tonight. Mr. Leggett, we'll bring the pennant back from the coast."

"It'll be more than that, Ben," the owner said. "You'll be bringing back the game the way it was meant to be played."

"We've all been waiting a long time for that, Mr. Leggett," Sam McCloud said.

By ten o'clock that night it appeared to the over forty thousand Cleveland fans that the celebration at the plush hotel had been a little premature. The Bees had stung the Gold Sox and Felipe Vila for four runs and were leading by two when the home team came in for their bats in the last of the eighth. Halfway to the dugout, Howie fell back on his heels when he heard a familiar gravelly voice. "Come on, kid, take charge, will you?" He swung his head toward the third-base boxes and saw Herb Sayre shaking a fist at him.

He yelled at the players, "Take the lead out! Let's go!"

Alex Brand, hitting sixth, laid down a bunt and beat it out by an eyelash, and the fans came to life. McIver struck out, but Ragoni singled through the middle, and then Macklin gave Iffy Oldam the nod to hit for Vila. Howie, the big crowd chanting, "Go! Go, Gold Sox!" followed Iffy and knelt in the on-deck circle, his eyes on the scoreboard. The Moguls were way out in front of the Blue Sox, 10-3. Every game now could be the difference.

Iffy popped it up to the infield and was automatically out, and Howie, his teeth set hard, dug in at the plate. The Bee infield moved back a little when their pitcher got two strikes on him. He clubbed at the letter-high pitch he expected, one designed to stop his bunt. The ball went through the middle, where the shortstop flagged it down, but there was no time for him to make a throw.

Howie yelled in at Ernenwine, then edged off first. The three runners were off when Ernenwine cut at the first pitch, but they had to come back when he fouled it off. The Kansas City left-hander held a conference with his catcher, and the thousands yelled for them to break it up and go on with the game.

Ernenwine hung in, fouling off half a dozen pitches after running the count two and two. He ran the string out, then connected with a fast outside pitch and rode it to the left-field corner, the base runners on the move with the crack of the bat.

Alex Brand scored. Ragoni was not far behind him with the tieing run, and then the huge crowd came up, screaming for Cy Turkin to hold Howie Patton up, for the little shortstop was not putting on the brakes as he neared third base. Out on the grass the Bee shortstop was about to glove the relay from the outfield. Howie wheeled around third, dead certain he was going to score, as sure of it as he was that the Gold Sox would never be headed off the rest of the way to the flag.

The throw came in. He hit the dirt, just as the Kansas City catcher lurched to his right a little to get the throw, then twisted his body away from the desperate tag. The umpire's safe call turned loose a deafening blast of sound that fanned out over the lake. The Gold Sox were out in front, 5-4.

Howie paused on the way to the dugout and tipped his cap, ostensibly to the wildly cheering fans, but it was really for those men sitting in the field box close to the Gold Sox bench, Sam McCloud and the others who had made the Little General what he was. Their big pleased grins told him that they knew, just before he ducked down out of sight.

ABOUT THE AUTHOR

Joe Archibald began his writing career at the age of fifteen with a prize-winning contribution to the Boston Post. At the age of twelve he submitted and sold his first cartoon to the original *Judge* Magazine. He is a graduate of the Chicago Academy of Fine Arts.

During World War I, he served on a subchaser for the United States Navy and was staff cartoonist for a service publication. After the armistice, he was a police and sports reporter for Boston newspapers, and then went to New York and became a sports and panel cartoonist for the McClure Newspaper Syndicate. In 1929 he began free-lancing, and since then has written countless stories and articles for boys —sports, aviation, adventure, etc. With the outbreak of World War II, Joe Archibald became a cartoonist for the American Theater Wing, and went overseas as a field director for the Red Cross.

His first book, published in 1947, won for him an enthusiastic following of young readers throughout the country, and the books he has written since then have proved his popularity with sports-minded boys.

He is a member of the National Cartoonists Society, has exhibited water colors, and is a director of amateur musical shows. He lives in Port Chester, N.Y., and is very active in community affairs.